FINAL FANTASY
THE SPIRITS WITHIN

FINAL FANTASY™
THE SPIRITS WITHIN

A NOVEL BY
DEAN WESLEY SMITH

BASED UPON
FINAL FANTASY: THE SPIRITS WITHIN

SCREENPLAY BY ALAN REINERT AND JEFF VINTAR

BASED ON AN ORIGINAL STORY BY
HIRONOBU SAKAGUCHI

POCKET BOOKS
NEW YORK   LONDON   TORONTO   SYDNEY   SINGAPORE

An *Original* Publication of POCKET BOOKS

POCKET BOOKS, a division of Simon & Schuster, Inc.
1230 Avenue of the Americas, New York, NY 10020

ISBN: 0-7434-2419-0

First Pocket Books printing July 2001

10 9 8 7 6 5 4 3 2 .

POCKET and colophon are registered trademarks of
Simon & Schuster, Inc.

Printed in the U.S.A.

FINAL FANTASY™

THE SPIRITS WITHIN

chapter 1

The dream was always changing, even though it always felt the same.

Aki jerked awake, coming up out of sleep like a swimmer gasping for breath. She brushed her shoulder-length hair out of her face and looked around the lab, letting the familiar surroundings ease the tension. She was strapped in her lounge chair in the research area of her ship. She was in orbit, headed for the right time and spot for reentry into the atmosphere.

She took a deep breath and let it out slowly. The dream felt the same, time after time, yet every time she had it there were subtle changes. Changes she knew meant something.

The dream haunted her like an echo as she tried to push the images aside. She reached for the holographic control panel over her chair. The display read:

Dream File Save? Yes? No? 12/13/2065

Aki punched *Yes* and the hologram disappeared. With a click, the scanning device retracted into the panel over her head and the magnetic connectors holding her in the chair deactivated. She floated upward in the zero gravity from the released pressure of her body on the chair.

The dream dug at her mind like a mole, trying to show her something. It always *felt* the same. Always. But she had decided to try recording them, to see what the differences really were, and if she could find out what they meant.

She pushed herself across the high-tech laboratory toward the window, letting the moment of floating in zero g ease her tension. Her quest had caused enough problems without her sleep being plagued by the dream. If the Council knew about her dreams, they would shut down her research, she was sure.

But she needed to know what the dreams meant.

She eased herself into an upright position near the port, grasping a handhold to stay in place as she stared at the blue and white of Earth hundreds of miles below. It was so beautiful, it calmed her even more, and set her resolve to understand what was happening.

She let the images of the dream come back.

An alien sun and a massive moon shone through a thick, dusty sky, at levels too bright for comfort. She was standing in a barren wasteland that was clearly scarred from a massive battle. Under her feet seemed to be a lake, yet she remained on the surface, her own image reflecting back at her, as if she was standing on a mirror.

She was waiting for something. She had no idea what.

Then, over the horizon, a light started to outshine the hot sun, adding to the feeling of intense heat.

She knew something was coming.

She could sense it, feel it in the shaking of the surface under her.

The air around her rumbled louder and louder; the dust, swirling like a breeze, was kicking it up. Yet she could feel no wind against her face, no movement of her hair.

Something big was coming.

Huge.

But she didn't know what.

She just waited, facing it, wanting to turn and run, yet not doing so. She needed to know what it was.

She needed to face it.

The air swirled, the dust choked her. The surface under her feet shook as the horizon got even brighter.

The unknown came closer.

And closer.

Then she had woken up, the dream over.

Most of the dream was the same as other times, but this time it felt as if she was closer to understanding.

It frustrated her that she could not see what was coming at her over that horizon. She felt she needed to know what it was, but she could think of no way to extend the dream. She would just have to wait, let the dream explain itself to her.

But waiting was not something she did easily.

She shook off the feeling of dread and tried to calm her fast-beating heart. Just thinking about the dream got her upset. She desperately needed to know what it meant. And what she was waiting for.

She stared out the portal. Below her Earth spun slowly, beautiful from orbit. She hoped beyond all hope that she would be in time to save her wonderful home planet.

"Atmosphere reentry in fifteen seconds," The *Black Boa*'s autopilot announced over the communication link, its metallic voice as calm as always. This was going to be a dangerous and tricky drop, and she needed to be clear and ready for it.

She pushed off the portal and floated up into the control cabin. Just as the chair there snapped her into position, the *Black Boa* bumped slightly and then leveled, the autopilot she had programmed taking her into the mission. Through the portal she could see red from the heat flaring off the hull as the ship sliced into the atmosphere. The pressure pushed her against the chair's restraints, but she ignored it. Now she had to think about the coming mission.

She was dropping in over the Atlantic, hot and fast, just as she had planned to do. It was dark where she was heading, the morning still over Eastern Europe, a long way from the East Coast of North America. With luck she would be in, get the sixth spirit, and be out before anyone, or anything, could even move to meet or stop her.

The thumps of the atmosphere reentry eased and she took a deep breath, forcing herself to relax. The feeling of gravity reassured her as she eased the ship in toward the target. She just hoped the sixth spirit was still there.

"Thirty seconds to landing," the autopilot said.

"Ready," she said to herself, ignoring the fact that she was talking to her ship's computer.

"Warning! This is restricted air space," the computer said.

She tapped her control board, overriding the restriction, not taking her eyes off the ground rushing up at her.

"Fifteen seconds."

She wanted to take the controls in her own hands, but it was now pitch-black outside the ship. It was better to let the computer land her, right where she had programmed it to.

"Five seconds."

She could see something moving past the ship on all sides in the darkness, but the blast of the ship's propulsion wasn't enough to light up what it was.

The ship bumped and then settled, and the engines shut off.

"Landing confirmed."

She quickly checked the details. The ship had brought her right where it was supposed to. Now, to get what she was here for and get out.

She snapped off the safety restraints of her chair and headed out of the control room. Stopping for only a few seconds in the lab to grab her equipment, she stepped toward the closed hatch and took a deep breath. She was going to make this work. She had no choice.

She tapped the control on the wall.

The hatch in front of her clanged and slid downward.

Nothing but blackness faced her. It was almost as if she were looking into the depths of space, without the stars.

The hatch snapped into a horizontal position, becoming a ramp as she stepped onto it.

She took the flare gun from her belt and aimed it up and away from the ship, then fired.

The orange and white light of the flare lit an incredible black world around her.

She knew it had been called Times Square.

She had seen pictures of this area in its heyday, long before her birth, when the parties celebrating the New Year would fill this area with millions of people. It had been an area of life, of activity.

Now there was only darkness and ruin. The sight hit her hard, right in the stomach, making her take a deep breath.

Crumbling buildings loomed over piles of brick, mortar, and rusted old cars. All the glass in all the windows was long gone, leaving the holes as empty, dead eyes, the blackness too deep to even think about. This was the same kind of destruction she kept seeing in her dreams. Only her dream was of an alien world; this was reality on *her* world.

She forced herself back to the task at hand, scanning the area around the ship for any sign of the Phantoms, lit up by the flare. Nothing.

She pulled out her gun, holding it ready as she moved down the last few meters to the ground. Dust and debris swirled away from her, caused by the motion of her feet. But even that little wind seemed wrong and out of place in this much death. She had no idea when the last time a human had been here was. Too long ago, that was certain.

With one more glance around the flare-lit ruins that

towered over her, she clicked on the scanner over her left eye. The faint beep seemed far louder in the deadness.

The flare died out and Aki fired another, aiming up between two of the tallest buildings. The flare exploded hundreds of meters above her ship, sending trailers of red and white. Her scanner confirmed no life-forms in the area, in any of the buildings at any level.

"All right," she said aloud, taking a deep breath as the hatch touched down. She stepped off onto a rough pile of rubble. "Where are you?"

Her bracelet scanner blinked as she held it up and slowly turned. On the display it read, "No life-form."

Turning degree by degree, she moved around, letting the scanner do its work. Then, as she faced to the south, the blinking increased and became steady.

"Got you," she said, her voice smothered by the darkness as the flare went out.

She shot another flare into the air to the south and scanned the area to make sure nothing was coming at her. So far it was still clear. She climbed off the pile of debris, moving down what had once been the center of a very busy street, climbing over or going around debris as she needed to.

Her footsteps were the only sounds. She could tell that what she was looking for was directly ahead, inside a building. She kept moving as fast as she dared in all the debris. At the top of one pile her flare was about to die out again, so she fired another.

This time the eye scanner caught something moving in the distance, down the street, as the flare exploded overhead.

Her heart seemed to stop as every nerve in her body froze. Suddenly the very dead city was no longer so dead. Out of open windows and shadows, her eye scanner showed her dozens of Phantoms, climbing into the street like animals coming from their dens.

She had seen Phantoms up close before. Invisible to the naked human eye, under the special energy flares they appeared. There were many kinds of Phantoms, but the ones she had just seen seemed grossly asymmetric creatures, translucent like glowing jellyfish. They had enormous heads and multi-tentacle arms. In the light of the flare they looked reddish.

They owned this old city.

She glanced back toward where the *Black Boa* was sitting, a familiar shape in the alien world of this ruined city. A half dozen of the Phantoms were coming out of holes between her and her ship.

She took a deep breath. She only had one choice, and that was to get the sixth spirit and get out quickly. She would never get another chance at it if she bailed out now.

With a quick check of her scanner to confirm where the sixth spirit was, she took off running, moving through the debris as fast as she could, her pistol held ready in case any of the Phantoms got too close.

As the flare overhead started to fade, she fired yet another, making sure she could see anything getting too close.

Ahead, in the open doorway of one giant building, a Phantom moved to face her. Her wrist scanner told her the sixth spirit was behind it, in that same building. She didn't dare fire at the Phantom for fear of hurting what she was here to find. Killing a thousand of these creatures was not worth what having the sixth spirit would be worth to humanity.

Suddenly a rumbling noise filled the dead canyons of buildings, and a bright light replaced the fading glow of her last flare. The rumbling got louder and louder, shaking the dust off everything around her.

She stopped and looked up. It took her a moment to realize what she was seeing—then she understood. It was a suborbital military transport ship coming in fast down one street, barely fitting between the tall buildings.

Clearly not only was she going to have trouble from the Phantoms, but from her own people as well.

Suddenly four soldiers in heavy armor dove from the transport as it flashed overhead, weapons held out in front of them as they headed for the ground.

Suddenly the four soldiers fired, and all around her high-density pellets hit the ground. Aki stayed still. She had seen this before, but never up close.

The pellets quickly exploded and spread, forming a thick cushion on the debris and concrete of the old street. She was completely surrounded.

The four came in hard and fast, rolling on the cushion as they hit and bouncing up, ready to fire.

Within seconds the cushion around them dissolved into thin air, quicker than it had formed. She knew enough about the military to know this was how they did emergency insertions. Diving from a fast-moving transport was not something they did lightly. They obviously considered her situation an emergency.

On the point man's armor was the name Deep Eyes.

She figured that must be the name of their platoon, because under the words Deep Eyes was the name Ryan.

Aki glanced around as the soldiers framed her. One was named Jane, another Neil, and their leader had nothing on his armor.

Neil fired a laser-type rifle just past her, and she spun around to see a Phantom hit. When the energy from the shot hit the alien, it discharged, making the Phantom almost white and clearly visible to the naked eye. Then the shot's energy caused the Phantom's structural integrity to break down. In other words, the shot vaporized it.

The other soldiers fired, hitting advancing Phantoms in all directions.

She fired another flare up into the air so she could see the Phantoms.

As the three kept firing, holding back the creatures, the leader turned to her, his face covered completely in the metal-gray armor, his voice amplified slightly. "This is a restricted area. Your ship has been impounded. Do not move."

"What's she doing here, Captain?" one of the soldiers shouted between shots.

"I don't know," the captain said as he fired and killed the Phantom blocking her path in the doorway, "but we're getting her out."

She had no intention of going with these soldiers until she had what she had come for. And there was nothing they could do to stop her.

Two Phantoms emerged from the doorway to the leader's left. "Behind you!" she shouted, pointing.

As the leader turned to fire, she sprinted for the now

cleared doorway, her wrist scanner showing her she was on the right track, her eye scanner telling her she wasn't running directly into the tentacles of a Phantom.

Behind her she heard the captain shout, "Halt! Dammit! I said halt!"

She knew he wouldn't fire on her, since she was the one they had come here to get.

She ducked through the doorway and snapped on a light attached to her eye scanner. Her light was enough to see the destruction in the massive space inside the building. This must have been a huge lobby at one time, with smooth floors and a vast ceiling three or four stories overhead. A large part of the building had broken away and fallen out to the west, showing the night sky above part of the room.

She fired a flare up into one corner. No Phantoms yet.

Outside she heard the captain shout, "Let's move, people!" Then the sharp crack of more firing.

She moved deeper into the building, following the direction the scanner told her to move. Behind her, the soldiers came in as well.

"Two coming through the east wall," one shouted.

She glanced to the right, seeing the two Phantoms as they were hit and vaporized just after coming into the huge lobby.

Suddenly the leader of the soldiers grabbed her arm and yanked her around. He'd come up on her fast and silent. "Just what the hell do you think you're doing?"

She stared into the armor-covered face, feeling she should know who was behind it. "There's a life-form in here."

"There hasn't been life here in years," the captain said, clearly not believing her.

"There is now," she said, indicating the blinking scanner on her wrist. "And it's right in here, somewhere close."

"Life-form or not," the leader said as the other soldiers spread out around him, guarding all the flanks, "I'm taking you in."

"Fine," she said. "Take me, I don't care. But not until I extract this life-form."

She yanked her arm out of the soldier's grasp and moved deeper into the building, following the signal on her scanner. She knew it had to be close. It was almost as if she was right on top of it.

"This is going to be one of those days," the captain said behind her. "Flank us."

Then, taking a position a half step behind her, he shone his brighter armor light ahead, staying with her step for step as they went deeper and deeper into the old building's lobby. She was surprised at the help, but said nothing.

Then she saw what she was after.

For a moment she couldn't believe it. At the base of what had been a large, clearly elaborate marble fountain, was her goal. It sat there, green against the gray and blackness of the old lobby.

She ran toward it, feeling more excited than she had in a long time.

"Captain," one of the soldiers said, "the transport is circling. It's not going to wait much longer."

"I understand that," the captain said, his voice echoing from right behind her.

She got to the edge of the fountain and kneeled down, while the captain shone his light on her find. It looked like a weed, growing up from a crack in the floor.

"It's in bad shape," Aki said to herself as she pulled out her extraction kit. She had known that the sixth spirit was going to be a plant, but until now she hadn't known what kind or how big.

"Oh, please," one of the soldiers said. "Tell me we're not risking our necks for this plant?"

"I wouldn't call it a plant," another soldier said. "It's more like a weed."

"I need just a minute to extract it," Aki said, focusing on what she was doing. She needed to cut a force field down through the concrete around the plant, making sure she got enough of it to keep the plant's roots completely intact.

"Miss," one of the soldiers to her left said, "that's a minute we don't have."

"I'm afraid he's right about that," another said.

She glanced around the massive room. They were right. In the light of her last flare she could see that Phantoms were coming through the walls like water through a strainer. She turned back to her task, working as quickly as she could. She would have to depend on the soldiers to give her the moments she needed.

"Take them out," the captain said.

The room echoed with laser fire, the sound rebounding and covering the distant rumble of the transport.

"We're not slowin' them down much," one soldier said.

"I'm afraid I agree, Captain," another said. "We need to get moving."

"Understood," the captain said. "Could you please hurry?"

Aki closed the force field around the plant and the small hunk of flooring and lifted the plant up into the air. "Done," she said, putting it in a protective-status pack on her side.

"About damn time," Jane said.

"Captain?" Neil said.

"Yeah," the captain said as he fired three quick shots in a row, taking out three of the Phantoms coming at them from the right.

"Just so you know," Neil said, "I agree with the 'let's get outta here' thing."

"Duly noted," the captain said.

Around them, all Aki could see was Phantoms. It seemed like a wall of them. And when one was destroyed, another seemed to flow into its place—a constantly moving wall of energy.

"Get into position," the captain said into his com link.

A moment later a bright light filled the hole in the roof over the lobby. The Phantoms around them didn't seem to notice at all as the transport moved into position.

One of the soldiers reached over and took the flare gun from Aki's belt. "Can I borrow this?" the soldier asked, snapping it onto the end of his rifle. "Thanks."

A moment later the flare gun lit up the room as the soldier shot round after round in three directions, illuminating the Phantoms even more than before.

"Shit, there's more then I thought," Ryan said.

"I hate to say I told you so," Neil said.

"We're surrounded," Jane said, her voice calm. "Ain't this a bitch."

The captain spun and killed two Phantoms trying to come at them over the fountain. "We've got to get to higher ground. Ryan, take point and clear a way toward those stairs on the right."

Ryan did as he was ordered, and the group, with Aki holding her gun up ready to fire, moved as a unit, blasting away at the Phantoms, killing enough of them to punch a hole through and keep the others away at the same time.

Aki could see what the captain was up to. Up the stairs was a clear space under the large opening in the roof. The ship could extract them there if they made it. Down here on the main floor, they were doomed.

The captain stepped past them, exchanging places with Ryan as they reached the bottom of the stairs. He did a quick inspection, then ordered. "Get up there. Jane, you take point. Make it one at a time, people."

Aki doubted the old, debris-covered stairs would even hold the weight of one soldier in armor, let alone all of them, but at the moment, the way the wave of Phantoms was closing in on them, they didn't have much choice.

Jane went up first, staying against the wall, moving quickly for a woman in so much armor. Neil went next, then Aki followed him, being careful to keep her footing and not slip. A tumble on this much debris at this slope might send her tumbling right down into the Phantoms.

Jane reached the top and moved to a position where she could lay down covering fire below. Neil took out three Phantoms coming in at them along the second floor.

Aki reached the landing and stopped, trying to look in all directions at once. She had been in a lot of tight spots before, but this was one of the worst. But the plant in her pouch was worth it. It just might be the key they needed to save the planet and stop this war.

Ryan reached the top of the stairs and stopped to cover the captain.

Aki watched in horror as three Phantoms started up behind him, moving far faster than the captain could move on the debris-covered stairs.

Ryan took out one.

The captain stopped and caught the other two just before they covered him. But the shots broke some of the rock and stone free above him. The rocks smashed him down, hard.

For a breathless moment Aki didn't think the captain would move, but then he was up, scrambling toward them as two more Phantoms bore down on him. He had lost his rifle, so it was up to Ryan to cover him.

Neil took Aki by the arm and moved them both closer to the top of the stairs as Jane took up a position near Ryan.

"When I say 'drop,' " Jane shouted, "you drop!"

"Drop!"

The captain went facedown on the staircase as two laser shots vaporized the two Phantoms behind him.

"Come on, Captain," Jane shouted. "You can make it."

As Aki watched the captain get back to his feet and

start up again, Neil started firing beside her, cutting down Phantom after Phantom coming at them through the walls and along the second-story landing.

At that moment the rubble that covered the upper area of the stairs started to slip, sending the captain to his knees again, headed right back down into the grasp of the Phantoms below him.

Jane snapped a safety hook and line on a banister with an expert flip, jumped down on the moving rubble and grabbed the captain's hand. With a yank, she pulled him upward with brute strength.

A moment later both of them scrambled to the top of the stairs.

"Too damn close," Jane said. "You okay?"

"Yeah," the captain said. "Fine."

"We're not out of this yet," Neil said, firing as fast as he could. "You two want to have the meeting later?"

"Kind of snippy, isn't he?" Jane said, turning and firing on three Phantoms coming through a wall at them.

Aki was impressed. These four clearly had worked together a long time, and were very calm under all kinds of pressure.

"They're coming en masse!" Ryan said.

Above her Aki saw four cables lowering into the open ceiling from the transport. With all their weapons firing, the leader stepped toward her, took her by the waist, and lifted her off the ground.

"Any time," Neil said as the mass of Phantoms bore down on them from all sides.

"Lift," the captain said.

She held his arm with one hand while her other hand made sure the plant was safe. Below them the mass of writhing Phantom tentacles reached up for them, barely missing their feet as the transport pulled them through the roof and up into the dark bay.

That was close. Just a little too close.

But she knew, without a doubt, it was going to be worth it if what she had was really the sixth spirit.

chapter 2

To Gray, the interior of the troop transport seemed crowded as the four of them and Aki got on board. It had never felt that way to him before, but just being this close to Aki bothered him.

He dropped into a seat in the back, as far away as he could get from the thin, beautiful woman they had just rescued. He kept on his helmet, because he didn't want her to see him yet. There was too much history between them, too much past. And far too many questions.

The rest of his team took off their head gear and stashed it under their seats as Aki carefully stored the force pack that held the plant she had been after. Gray knew she was damned lucky to be alive. Actually, they all were. Just one touch of those Phantom tentacles and they would have been infected. And once infected, there wasn't much hope. The empty city of old New York proved that. Once those aliens got you, you were a goner.

"You okay?" Ryan asked Aki as she finished securing her treasure and dropped into a seat facing them all. Ryan was one of the most capable members of his squad, the proverbial "strong, silent" type, an effective leader who always looked out for the other members of the team.

Aki smiled and nodded to Ryan that she was all right. That smile made the emotions inside Gray boil. He had thought that, after this much time had passed, he had put the desire away, but his feelings for Aki were still with him. And right now, anger played a large part in those feelings.

Anger and hurt and betrayal. She had left him— without a word or reason—and had refused to even take his calls. He had never been put through anything like it before.

"Can you give me one reason," Gray said, his helmet still on, his voice altered by the transmitter, "why I shouldn't arrest you?"

Aki stiffened. She always did that when pressed. Gray knew the reaction well. She would defend herself and attack if she had to. And right now he just didn't care. He wanted her to be angry, to be just as hurt as he was.

"I am Doctor Aki Ross." She looked at Gray with eyes daring him to challenge her. "I have clearance to be here."

Gray laughed. "You and I both know it's not unlimited clearance, and you couldn't go where you did without authorization."

Gray knew that for a fact. He had checked when they were on the way, after her ship had been spotted dropping into the old city. At first, when he had gotten the information, he hadn't believed it was her ship; but then the fact that it *was* her made him push his people even more. And it had almost gotten them killed. He had let his emotions jeopardize his squad, and that made him even angrier. Both at himself and her.

Aki glared at him. "Listen, Captain, I don't have the time for this."

"Do you realize," Gray said, "that you just risked the lives of my squad, and mine?"

Aki stood and turned her back on him, checking her prize plant with her bracelet scanner. Then she turned back to face him, her eyes slitted and angry.

"Look, I don't want to talk about it," she said. "The fact of the matter is, it was *worth* the lives of you and your men."

There was a very awkward silence in the cabin.

Outside the cabin, Gray could see that the transport had crossed over the barrier enclosing the new city of New York and was heading for a landing at the military entry gate. At night the massive, bubble-like barrier that protected millions of humans sparkled like stars and glowed a faint orange. Normally he liked looking at it, but at the moment he wasn't enjoying anything.

"You and your men?" Jane said under her breath, shaking her head in disgust. Gray knew she hated to be thought of as a man, even though she was tougher than anyone else in his squad.

"She thinks you're a man," Ryan said, smiling at Jane.

"It's the suit," Neil said.

"I think she's an idiot," Jane said, loud enough for Aki to hear.

"I know you're not a man," Neil said to Jane.

"I think you're an idiot, too," Jane said.

Gray unclipped his helmet as he talked. "Well, I *do* wanna talk about it, Dr. Ross. Sometimes, whether you like it or not, other people have to be involved with what you do. Did it ever occur to you, *Doctor*, that maybe we would have *volunteered* to risk our lives?"

"Well," Aki said, glaring at him, "nobody asked you to save me."

Gray shook his head. That was just like the old Aki he knew. Stubborn and defensive, right down to the last. "You know, you have not changed one bit."

Aki stared at him.

Gray nodded to her, then reached up and took off his helmet, storing it under his seat before looking up into the shocked, beautiful eyes of his old love. The same love that had left him suddenly and without reason.

"Gray?" Aki said, her voice barely above a whisper.

At that moment the transport touched down.

"Yeah," Gray said, staring at her. It was everything he could do to keep his face blank, his emotions inside, locked up where he had kept them since she had left. "Nice to see you, too."

Aki could not believe it had been Gray and his squad who had saved her. The discovery had shocked her right to her core, and brought up all the feelings for him she thought she had put away. The feelings she didn't have time for.

Somehow, as they unloaded out of the transport, she managed to not look at or say anything to him.

And he said nothing to her. Clearly he was angry at her, and had every right to be. But she didn't trust herself enough to tell him what was happening. It had been better, and easier, to just leave him, not even saying good-bye. There just hadn't been time.

Now, seeing him again brought up all the doubts about that decision.

"Welcome back, Captain," a lab technician said to Gray as they entered the decontamination area through the ship's airlock.

"Good to be back, Dan," Gray said.

Aki glanced around. This place was just like all the decontamination areas at the barrier entrances. Everything was a pure white; no color at all was allowed in the room.

A glass-like partition divided them from the tech and an emergency medical area behind him. There was only a round platform on their side of the partition. The scanner was what it was called, because that was what it did. It scanned a person for alien infestations. No alien spirit was allowed through this room.

She didn't dare go through the scanning. Her secret would be revealed to Gray and everyone else in the room, and she couldn't have that happen.

She looked around, trying to figure a way out of this. She had been infested by an alien while doing an experiment, and Dr. Sid had found a way to contain it, keep it from killing her. But the alien spirit was still inside her, just waiting to break out, and only a few at the top levels of security knew that fact. She had no doubt the tech and Gray were not in that need-to-know group.

The infestation contained inside her was the reason

she had left Gray. And now, if she didn't do something quickly, he would know, and her cover would be broken for sure. And having her cover broken might end what she was doing to save the planet.

"We're clean," Gray said.

"I can vouch for that," Aki said, hoping the tech would just let them pass.

Dan smiled back at them while adjusting something on a panel in front of him. "Let's make sure of that, shall we? From the record of your little adventure, you got damned close to a few of them."

Behind Aki all three of the Deep Eye squad moaned as one.

"I hate gettin' scanned," Neil said.

"The scanners are probably worse for us than the Phantoms," Ryan said, annoyed.

"No probably about it," Neil said. "These machines are suspected of causing sterility and I wanna have a little Neil, Jr. calling me Daddy someday."

"That's a damn spooky thought," Jane said, staring at Neil.

"Why are you always bustin' my chops?" Neil asked, staring back at her.

Aki said nothing. There was no doubt that the scanners were far better than being infected by a Phantom. She should know. But at the moment she had no idea how she was going to get out of being scanned. There was only one door out of this room, and that was through a shimmering force screen on the other side of the scanner.

"People!" Gray said in a sharp command tone. "Let's just do this thing."

"Yes, sir!" all three of the squad said at the same time.

Ryan stepped up onto the platform and smiled at Dan. "Scan away."

Dan nodded, and on the monitor over Ryan's head appeared a wavering image of blue. It shimmered on the screen like a heat wave coming off a hot desert road.

The technician studied the image and readouts on his board for a moment to be sure, but Aki knew with a glance at the monitor that Ryan was clean. She had been studying spirit images for so long now she knew every detail of how a human image looked, and where alien spirits could hide.

"Okay, next," Dan said.

Ryan stepped down and moved through the shimmering entrance to the other side of the barrier, looking very bored the entire time.

Jane stepped up and took his place on the scanning pad.

Neil glanced up at the blue shimmering image of her spirit on the screen. "Looks like you've gained some weight."

Jane shook her head. "It's called upper body strength. Christ, Neil, get a girlfriend."

"I'm working on it," Neil said, smiling at her.

"You're clear," Dan said, and Jane stepped down and went to join Ryan through the shield, letting Neil take her place.

Aki stepped up beside Gray. "You know my security rating allows me to bypass this."

Gray frowned, but didn't turn to look at her. "Not today it doesn't."

"You're clean," Dan said to Neil.

Neil joined the other members of the squad through the barrier beside Dan as Gray stepped up on the platform.

Aki had to do something. This test was more dangerous to her than the Phantoms had been. "Listen, Captain," she said to Gray, "I think we—"

"I don't care what you think, Doctor," Gray said, the anger just below the surface of his voice, his eyes focused directly on her. "You're getting scanned just like the rest of us."

Aki was just about to say he was dead wrong and that she had no intention of being scanned when an alarm filled the room, cutting off all sound in a high-pitched scream.

Gray and the rest of his squad crouched, hands on their weapons, as a cylinder dropped from the ceiling and circled Gray, trapping him and holding him in place.

It took a second for Aki to understand what had happened; then, with a glance at the red mingled with the blue of Gray's spirit on the monitor, she knew.

Gray was infested.

"Aw, shit!" Ryan said.

"Captain?" Jane said, stepping toward him. She was stopped by the clear wall.

"They got him!" Neil said.

"There must be a mistake," Gray shouted. "Nothing touched me!"

"Sorry, sir," Dan said, his attention focused on the board in front of him. "You came in contact with a Phantom. Please stay calm in there. I'm administering a treatment shield."

Gray took a deep breath and stood up straight, facing this as he would face any battle. It was that strength that Aki had loved in him. And right now he was going to need all the strength he had.

Aki stepped up to the glass and scanned the data on the tech's board on the other side. "What level is he?"

"Blue," Dan said.

Her stomach twisted into a knot. He was very advanced. The infestation must have happened early on, maybe in the street when they first dropped in. A Phantom touch infected. If a Phantom went through you, it robbed you instantly of life.

"It'll be code red in three minutes, twenty seconds," Dan said.

Code red meant that Gray was basically dead. At code red, the Phantom particles became part of the human spirit, no matter how little of them were in the body. It was a transformation that she and Dr. Sid did not yet fully understand. The only way to save Gray now was to get those Phantom particles out of him in the next three minutes.

Aki glanced at the setting behind the tech. "Is that a full operating lab, and is everything working?"

"It is," the tech said, his fingers working over his board, doing what he could for Gray.

Aki knew that a medical team was headed here at top speed, but they would be too late. Gray didn't have the time or any second chance. Not like she had had.

"We have to treat him now!" Aki said to the tech.

"I'm sorry," Dan said, shaking his head, "but that's impossible. We'll transfer him to the Treatment Center."

Aki glanced at the tech, then turned to The Deep Eye

squad on the tech's side of the barrier. "He doesn't have time for that. I might be able to save him back there."

It took Jane and Ryan only a moment to understand what she was saying. Jane moved over and stood over the small frame of the tech. He looked up at her, then nodded. Then, with a quick glance at the board, he dropped the barrier and lifted the cylinder that was holding Gray.

"Shit, you've done it now," Gray said.

"Shut up and get on that table," Aki ordered, motioning for Ryan to help him. She turned to Dan. "Seal this lab and keep it sealed. If I can't save him, I don't want a breach."

He nodded, smiled up at Jane, and then went back to working his board.

Ryan had Gray up on the operating table as Aki stepped to his side. She had worked these machines a hundred times. This would be no different. She couldn't let herself think about it being Gray in her hands.

She took the anesthetic gun and moved to put him under.

"Aki," Gray said, "there's something I need to say."

She put the gun to his neck and fired, the drug going into his blood with a faint hiss. "Don't try to speak."

The anesthetic kicked in almost instantly, and Gray closed his eyes.

"Here we go," she said, letting the table flash a holographic image of Gray's spirit over his body. What should be blue, showing the shimmering color of health, was being eaten away by red tentacles.

Alien spirit particles.

The tentacles writhed grotesquely, turning the blue particles of Gray's spirit red as they spread.

"Oh, shit," one of the squad said softly, seeing the image of their commander under attack.

"Would you look at that thing?" another said.

Aki was doing just that. She was carefully planning her attack on it. She had to get it all. Not one tiny piece of the Phantom could be left if she was going to save his life. "How much time?"

The tech flicked on a holo-image of a clock beside Gray. It read two minutes and twenty seconds.

"There's not enough time," the tech said. "When he reaches code red, the treatment shield over that table won't be able to hold the alien particles."

Aki knew that. She knew what would happen to Gray at that point as well. But she didn't have the time to tell the tech that. She activated the laser scalpel and went after the side of the red tentacle displayed on the holo image of Gray.

The laser wasn't actually cutting flesh, but something more important inside of Gray. This laser was designed to cut at the spirit of a subject. And in this case, the invading alien spirit. She had to cut it out, as well as all the infected parts of Gray's spirit.

She worked as fast as she could, moving around the edges of the red tentacle, keeping it contained, cutting it back from all sides as it tried to move out of her path.

It was like a dance with a twisting, fast-moving snake. It jumped, she was there ahead of it to cut it back. It moved another way, and she caught it.

She could feel sweat forming on her forehead. The medical team and security personnel were banging on one door, demanding to be let in. She ignored it all and just kept cutting.

Fraction by fraction, the red vanished from the holo-image.

"One minute," the tech announced, knowing Aki had not had the time to even glance at the holo-clock.

Finally she was down to just one small tentacle, but as she went after it, the thing seemed to vanish into the deepest blue of Gray's spirit.

"What's going on?" Ryan demanded. "Did you get it?"

"Where'd it go?" Jane asked.

Aki knew she hadn't gotten the last little tentacle. When pushed, the things always burrowed deeper and deeper into the host spirit.

And she was going to have to find it and go after it.

Her fingers danced over the controls of the holo-imager, searching through the blue of Gray's spirit for the last red tentacle. She had to track it like a dog hunting a wanted criminal, then trap it and destroy it before it reached Stage Red. If it did, it would be able to move anywhere, into any of them, through the medical shield around Gray.

And Gray would be finished if that happened.

Gray suddenly went into a light convulsion, his back arched.

"Infestation has gone deep," the tech said.

"Tracking," Aki said.

Following the holo image was like watching the passing landscape on a high-speed train flashing through a barely lit tunnel. But she had done it so many times before, she knew exactly what she was looking for.

"There's no time," Dan said.

"Tracking," Aki said.

"Everyone out of here!" Dan shouted. "Now!"

On the holo-image, Gray's spirit twisted and spun as if in agony, insane motions as the alien presence got closer and closer to Code Red.

"We're not moving," Jane said.

"His treatment shield is going to fail!" Dan shouted.

"You leave if you want," Neil said, his voice cold and firm. "But we're staying right here."

Suddenly, on the holo-image, among all the insane motions of a soul in agony, Aki saw the flash of red and honed in on it, chasing it, burning it, cutting it down until finally there was no red left.

An instant later the alarm sounded, indicating Code Red, turning the room to a nasty tint of red.

Then, before anyone could even move, the all clear was given and the room flashed back to its white color.

She had gotten it all. She stared at the wonderful blue of Gray's spirit as it slowly calmed and moved back to its natural form. It was as it should be.

"You got it?" Ryan asked.

All Aki could do was nod.

"Shit, that was close," Jane said.

"Too close," Neil said.

"Man, you're good," Dan said. "I've seen a dozen of those operations and never one done that fast."

"We didn't have much choice," Aki said.

"You got that right," Dan said, going back to his panel and releasing the security lockout.

Aki stared at the sleeping face of the man she loved

more than anything on the planet, the man she had left. She could never have let him die, anymore than he could let her die once he knew she was in the old city. She should have told him what she needed to do.

She should tell him everything. But that would mean long talks and the possibility of him hating her and the alien spirit she had trapped inside her body.

She could not deal with that now.

She had important work to do.

Maybe, at some time in the future—if there *was* a future for her and the rest of the human race—she would explain to him why she had left. She would tell him about the alien particles filling her, threatening her every moment of life.

She would tell him after it was gone.

Gray groaned, and his eyes fluttered open.

She stepped back as the members of his squad crowded around their captain, helping him sit up. Gray was shaking like an old man, but that was normal for a person who just had their very spirit invaded and cut at. He would recover fully.

Gray looked at Aki. For a moment she wanted to step to his side and comfort him, then she stopped herself. "It's all right, Captain," she said. "You'll be back to normal in no time."

Aki turned away, making sure the plant she had risked so much for was still in its container strapped to her hip. In front of her the door slid open as the security locks were released, and Dr. Sid, the man who had saved her life, walked into the room.

She tapped the container holding the plant and smiled at him.

Dr. Sid, a white-bearded man with a completely bald head, nodded that he understood.

"Ah, Doctor?" Dan said from near Gray and the rest of The Deep Eyes squad. "We still need to scan you for infestation."

"That won't be necessary," Dr. Sid said. "I'll take the responsibility."

"Yes, sir," Dan said.

"Hey, Doc," Ryan said, "thanks for saving the captain."

Aki nodded. "Thanks for the help in the old city."

Then, with a glance at Gray, she turned and left beside Dr. Sid. There was so much she wanted to say to Gray. But this just wasn't the time, or the place.

She hoped someday soon, if she and the rest of the planet survived, there would be time. She was going to do everything in her power to make that happen.

chapter 3

Aki walked beside Dr. Sid in silence as they headed toward the science labs through the well-lit corridors. The plant in its protective stasis-field container bounced lightly on her hip as she moved, reminding her at every step how close she had come to causing the death of the man she loved. She knew her mission was worth risking lives, but she had never intended to risk Gray's life, only her own.

"Are you all right?" Dr. Sid asked as they went through a security checkpoint, turned a corner of one hallway, and started down a long, almost empty hallway. This area was the secure science area, her home for the last few months. Very few scientists had access. She was one of the lucky ones, if she considered having an alien spirit trapped inside her lucky.

"The military impounded my ship," Aki said, not wanting to tell him about how she was feeling at the moment, or any of her thoughts about Gray. Dr. Sid had enough on his mind without her emotional problems as well.

Dr. Sid just nodded. They both knew that having the military impound her ship was a minor thing. They would have it back shortly. But Aki was thankful that Dr. Sid did not push the question.

A few moments later they turned into a brightly lit lab full of the latest, high-tech computers. The two of them had been spending most of their time in this lab, working to find the answer to the alien spirits that they were sure would save Earth.

Betty, Dr. Sid's aide and right hand, looked up from one work area and smiled as they entered. She was young, thin, and beautiful, and very brilliant. More than once she had helped with the brainstorming of ideas between Aki and Dr. Sid. She had been the doctor's aide for years now, and had no desire to move to any other post.

"Good to see you are all right," Betty said to Aki.

"Thanks," Aki said, unhooking the plant container from her belt.

"You got it?" Betty asked, her eyes brightening at the sight of the plant.

"Got the plant," Aki said, holding up the container. "Now to check if it's the *right* one."

"Forward me the Phantom data," Dr. Sid said to Betty, "and everything regarding the five spirits we've collected so far."

"Yes, Doctor," Betty said, quickly moving back to her computer.

"Spirits?" Aki asked, laughing as she put the plant

carefully on the lab table under the large sensor. "I thought we weren't supposed to use the 'S' word."

Dr. Sid shook his head, then said, "Don't get smart with me."

Over the main lab table the holographic images of the five spirits they had already collected came into being as Betty transferred the data from what they called the spirit holding tank. The spirits swirled and twisted around each other, forming an incomplete picture. There were still empty, black spaces in the flowing blue image, but to Aki, it was beautiful.

"Now, let's see if that plant does the trick." Dr. Sid scanned the small plant Aki had risked so much to get. It wasn't easy to extract a living entity's spirit, but it could be done.

As she watched, the holographic image of the plant's spirit formed above it, then, carefully, Dr. Sid moved the image toward the others.

As if it had always fit, the plant's spirit joined the other five, filling part of the black spaces exactly, flowing with the other spirits as if it had always been there.

Aki knew that the image in the air that now seemed even brighter and stronger was the opposite of a Phantom spirit image. Almost, that is. Now, with the addition of the spirit from the plant, it was closer. Much closer.

"It's a match!" Aki shouted, staring at the wonderful vision in front of them. "We've found it!"

"Yes," Dr. Sid said, nodding and staring at the readouts. "The sixth spirit."

"Beautiful," Betty said, moving over and standing beside Aki.

Aki stared at the six spirits as they formed a larger, far more complex image. She couldn't believe how fantastic it was. With each added spirit, the whole seemed to grow, gaining far more than was added.

"It was worth it," Aki said to herself, not taking her gaze off the spirits. She wanted, almost needed to make herself believe that even if she had lost Gray, this would have been worth it. But thank heavens she hadn't lost him.

"I suppose it was worth it," Dr. Sid said, "but you know your little scene today broke nearly every protocol?"

"Oh-oh, lecture time," Betty said, smiling at Aki before moving back across the room to her computer station.

Aki shrugged and pointed to the little plant whose spirit now mingled with the others. "How long do you think this would have survived outside the barrier?"

She stared at Dr. Sid as he finished his work with the sixth spirit, saying nothing. She had had to go in that way. The moment they had spotted the sign that this spirit was there, in old New York, she had known she had no other choice. She just hadn't planned on Gray risking his life to help her.

Dr. Sid finished with his work and turned to her, his face serious, as if he needed to say something very important. She had seen that look only a few times before.

"Aki, you know there are elements in the Council and military just waiting for an excuse to shut us down."

"Look," Aki said, not letting him go on, "twenty years

ago, who discovered this energy in the phantoms? You, that's who."

Dr. Sid shook his head. "The past. Today is—"

"Yeah, right," Aki said. "You also proved that the same life force existed in humans and every life-form, and thus made it possible to harness that energy for ovo-pacs, scanners, even the barrier that protects us."

Dr. Sid said nothing.

"Don't you think the Council knows all that?" Aki went on, making sure he got her point. "They trust you, and we're so close to solving this entire mess."

"We still need this part and that part. . . ." Dr. Sid said, pointing to the two remaining black areas in the spinning hologram of six spirits.

"Exactly," Aki said. "Just two more pieces and we'll have solved the puzzle."

"And we need to be free to find those pieces." Dr. Sid moved over toward his desk, tucked against the wall.

"You don't think they are going to give us that freedom?" Aki asked. She could not believe that the Council would be so stupid as to stop them now. Not when they were this close. Not after everything Dr. Sid had done for humanity so far.

"I have my doubts." Dr. Sid unlocked the top drawer of his desk and rummaged around in the back for a moment. "I want to show you something."

He held up a small, linen-bound book. It was clearly old and very well-used. He tossed it to Aki, then shut the desk drawer.

The book felt heavy in her hand. And yet soft and often-handled. "What is this?"

"Read."

She opened the book to the first page. It was covered in Dr. Sid's flowing handwriting.

"All life is born of Gaia, and each life has a spirit. Each new spirit is housed in a physical body."

Aki looked up at him. This looked like old notes of his. Why did he want her to read them now? And why about the idea that Earth was a mighty spirit called Gaia? "Doctor?"

"Go on."

She looked at the intense seriousness in his eyes, then nodded and went back to reading. "Through their experiences on Earth, each spirit matures and grows. When the physical body dies, the mature spirit, enriched by its life on Earth, returns to Gaia, bringing with it the experiences, enabling Gaia to live and grow."

"It's my old diary," Dr. Sid said. "I wrote that forty-three years ago, when I was the age you are now."

He took the book gently back from her, looked at it for a moment, then turned and tossed it into the small lab incinerator used to burn old experiments.

"Doctor!" Aki said. "Don't!"

It was too late. The sound of burning and the green light appearing on the face of the small machine confirmed that the book had been destroyed.

Dr. Sid faced Aki, his face very calm and stern. "Remember your history? Remember what happened to Galileo?"

Aki nodded. "They wouldn't do that to you."

"They would," Dr. Sid said. "They threw Galileo in jail because he said the Earth was not the center of the universe. It could happen to us as well. Our ideas are very unpopular."

"I know that," Aki said, still feeling stunned that he had destroyed his old notes.

"Good, I'm glad you do," he said. He pointed to his head. "Keep everything up here. Destroy any notes or records that might be used against you."

She stared at him for a moment, then slowly nodded. Things were getting worse. Faster than she had expected if the doctor was taking these kinds of precautions.

"I'll do it now," she said, turning toward her office.

"Good. And then come back here and we'll add the sixth spirit into the vest."

Aki touched the vest that encased her entire upper body under her clothes. It wasn't really a vest, more like a body wrap. A very high-tech one, that kept the alien infestation encased inside her, not allowing it take her over. With each new spirit, her defensive vest got a little stronger. When they found the last spirit, it would take the phantom out of her, neutralize it.

"It will take me a little while," she said.

"Just make sure you don't miss anything," Dr. Sid said, tossing more notes into the incinerator. "And stay away from your friend, the captain."

Aki stopped and turned back to Dr. Sid. "What?"

Dr. Sid laughed. "He saves your life, you save his. I was young once. One thing leads to another, you know."

Aki shook her head, stunned that Dr. Sid knew about her and Gray. They had kept their relationship very, very quiet. She glanced at the swirling image of the six spirits, then back at her mentor and friend. "Doctor, there's a war going on."

"I'm aware of that, *Doctor*," he said.

She looked at him, her gaze as cold as she could make it. "No one is young anymore."

With that, she turned and headed for her office to destroy the records of years' worth of work. If doing that meant surviving and finding the answers to saving Earth, than she would do it. And do it gladly.

chapter 4

The dream that night started off the same as every time before.

The hot sun and a massive moon shone through a thick, dusty sky, at levels too bright for comfort. Aki was standing in a barren wasteland that was clearly scarred from a massive battle. Under her feet seemed to be a lake, yet she remained on the surface, her own image reflecting back at her as if she was standing on a mirror. Around her the rest of the land was bone-dry and very dusty.

That was the same, the feelings were the same, the images exact. She had been here a hundred times before.

She was waiting for something. She had no idea what.

Yet she waited.

Then, over the horizon, a light started to outshine the sun and the moon.

Again, the same as always. She knew something was coming.

She could sense what was coming, feel it in the shaking of the surface under her.

The air around her rumbled louder and louder; the dust, swirling like a breeze, was kicking it up. Yet she could feel no wind against her face, no movement of her hair.

Something big was coming.

Huge.

Every time, every dream it happened. She felt exactly the same way each dream, but now this dream felt more real. All she could do was wait, facing whatever it was, wanting to turn and run, yet not doing so.

She needed to face it.

Somehow she knew that now. That had changed.

The air swirled, the dust choked her. The surface under her feet shook as the horizon got even brighter.

The unknown came closer.

And closer.

Then, at the point she had awoken the last time, she did not.

The dream progressed.

The dream changed.

Over the horizon an army of thousands of screaming aliens swarmed toward her. Somehow she knew they were Phantoms, yet they didn't look like the energy Phantoms she was familiar with. These were real aliens, in shiny armor, carrying weapons.

They were two-legged and came on like a wind from the center of hell.

Aki stood her ground as the earth trembled.

Then another rumbling was added to the first.

The very air around her seemed as if it might shake into nothingness. She turned to see a second alien army hurling itself at the first army.

This army was also in metallic armor, but they were shaped differently, with different-looking weapons.

She wasn't the point of the attack.

They were attacking each other. Not her.

She knew, without understanding how she knew, that she was standing in the middle of a battle in the war that had destroyed this alien place.

The screaming grew and grew, as if a thousand birds had combined with a thousand human children in terror, creating a noise that cut through her like knives. She held her head, trying to block the sound, but the noise only increased as the two armies swarmed closer and closer, surrounding her.

Then, just as the two are about to collide in battle, Aki woke up.

Beside her bed the alarm was buzzing gently. Her entire body was shaking and her legs were wrapped in the light blanket. It felt as if she had just sprinted miles.

She lay there, trying to catch her breath, her eyes open for fear that closing them might send her back into the dream. But the images were still with her, as real as if she had actually been there. There was no forgetting them.

But the real question was, what did they *mean*?

Could those armies she had seen actually be two different armies of Phantoms? The idea made her shudder. What about all the other types of Phantoms that now roamed the Earth? Where did they fit in?

And why now did the dream finally show her this battle? Was it the extra spirit in her vest defense? That was the only change since the day before. Could the addition of more spirits be taking her closer to the Phantoms instead of in the other direction? Clearly her dreams were becoming more real-feeling, and happening more often with each additional spirit in her shield.

That thought made her shudder even more. She couldn't let that kind of thinking stop her. She had work to do.

A lot of work.

There were two more spirits to find.

She rolled over and flipped off the alarm, then headed to clean up. Dr. Sid wanted her beside him in the Council meeting in one hour. And she needed to tell him about her dream first. Maybe he would understand it.

She hoped so. She sure didn't.

chapter 5

Gray sat four rows behind General Hein and watched as the Council members came in through a hidden door and took their seats. The council hall was one of those places that made Gray feel small. Thirty-four years before, when the Leonid Meteor had smashed into Earth, carrying the Phantoms, the Council had been formed from what was left of Earth's governments to coordinate the efforts to hold humanity together. At first they didn't have much luck, especially with the Phantoms spreading out all over the planet.

Then Dr. Sid had made his discoveries, which allowed the barriers to be built and places for the remains of humanity to safely go. During that early time, the Council had gained more and more power.

By the time Gray was born, the Council effectively ruled everything, in conjunction with a powerful military. The old national borders were long gone. Only the cities inside the barriers remained.

The council chamber had been built in New York—not the old New York City, where he had pulled Aki and her plant to safety, but in new New York, behind the largest barrier in the world, which protected millions. The Council chamber itself was a high-tech, massive space, with audience seating halfway around in a hundred-row-high balcony.

The eight-member Council sat on a high dais halfway up the open wall across from the audience. Anyone coming in to talk before the Council stood or sat at tables across from them. That was where Aki and Dr. Sid now sat as the council session began.

The military also had a position, to the right and lower than the council members. That was where Gray was seated, along with a dozen other officers.

Gray had never seen a council meeting where the military was not in attendance. A dozen times since becoming captain and leading the elite squad known as Deep Eyes, he had been asked to join the military contingent. Today he was here, he was sure, because of his involvement yesterday in old New York.

When Aki and Dr. Sid entered, Gray had felt as if his heart might pound right out of his chest. Just the sight of her brought back all the feelings he had for her. And yesterday he had saved her life, then she had saved his. Yet she still hadn't told him why she had left him, what he had done wrong. And that rejection by the woman he loved, and by a woman who clearly still loved him, ate at him. He had to know why.

As the Council took its seats and the session

opened, General Hein, one of the most powerful men in all the military, rose in front of Gray to speak. Hein was a short, broad-shouldered man who seemed intent on wiping the Phantoms off Earth single-handedly. Gray didn't much like him, but the general got things done, and in a time of war, that was all that mattered.

Aki looked over, and at that moment Gray could see her gaze move behind the general up to him. For an instant she almost seemed to smile. Then a frozen look came over her and she looked away.

"Ladies and gentlemen of the Council," General Hein said, "could you please explain why nothing has been done?" His words seemed to echo through the vast chamber, silencing even the light murmur of small talk in the audience.

In the middle of the vast room a holographic image of Earth and the space station came into being, controlled by a holographic panel in front of General Hein. The space station had been built ten years before, to hold position right over the Leonid Meteor crater. Gray had never been to the station, but he knew that it was a vast weapon, designed only to fight Phantoms right where they lived.

"Zeus was completed a month ago," General Hein said as, from the space station hologram, a beam was fired at the Earth below. "If we attack the meteor with this weapon, we will eliminate the Phantoms at their home. Why hasn't this been done?"

On the holographic image, the Zeus beam hit the meteor in the crater, eliminating it effortlessly.

Gray wondered the same thing. Why hadn't the weapon they had spent so much time and money to build been used? Aki had tried to explain to him that destroying the meteor and Phantoms wouldn't really happen the way the military engineers wanted. She couldn't say what might happen, but she was insistent that if General Hein was to be given permission to fire his weapon, there was no telling what damage could be done.

Those conversations had been back in the days when they were still talking, still holding each other, still sharing their lives. It hadn't been that long ago, but right now it felt to Gray like a lifetime had passed.

"So, esteemed Council, I would like an answer to my question. We have built the weapon that could save our planet. Why not use it?"

"We are here today to vote on that very issue," Councilwoman Hee said, her voice sharp and controlled.

Gray liked Hee most of all the Council, but he knew General Hein hated her. She seemed to be the strongest-willed, and the one not controlled by Hein and the military. And where Hee's votes went, so went many other council members'. Gray knew she drove General Hein crazy at times.

General Hein sat down, his back ramrod straight.

Gray started at the back of the general's head. He didn't seem old enough to be a general. Gray didn't feel old enough to be a captain and lead The Deep Eyes, yet he was. It was a time of war, and the young had to grow up fast.

"I'd like to ask the Director of the Bio-Etheric Center to speak," Councilwoman Hee said. "Dr. Sid, please."

Dr. Sid stood, and a holographic control panel appeared in the air like a podium in front of him. The image of the space station vanished as the holo-image filling the area in front of the Council zoomed down in toward the meteor crater.

"Thank you," Dr. Sid said. "As you all know, the Phantom's nest is in the Leonid Meteor."

Gray watched as, over the image of the meteor crater, another image was imposed.

"What you are seeing," the doctor said, "are the records of every assault on the Leonid Meteor to date. Putting it simply, physical attacks have had no effect."

The images scanned quickly through smaller bombs fired at the crater back when Gray was young, then larger and more concentrated attacks ten years before, until finally an atomic bomb had been dropped into the crater five years ago. At that, the image froze for a moment.

Numbers appeared beside the images. It was clear the numbers indicated Phantoms. After each attack the number dropped, then came quickly back to a stable place. Gray knew about this factor. Dr. Sid was not telling them anything new.

"This scene took place three months ago," the doctor said, "during a full-scale bombardment."

The image again went into motion as Bio-Etheric beams were fired at the Phantom nest. Basically those beams were smaller versions of the Zeus weapon. Gray watched as thousands of Phantoms were destroyed.

"Please note," Dr. Sid said, "the Phantoms outside and inside the meteor are indeed destroyed. However, deep under the meteor, many that were dormant seem to come to life."

Gray watched as the numbers showing how many Phantoms were alive dropped, then came back up. Gray remembered being very depressed the day of that attack.

"As you see, overall Phantom density remains the same, as it always does. And the newly risen aliens respond to the attack by burrowing even deeper into the Earth."

Councilwoman Hee stopped Dr. Sid. "This is very interesting," she said, "because we see the same thing during surgery when using Bio-Etheric lasers on Phantom particles, do we not? The alien particles go deeper."

Gray knew she was right. His team had shown him the replay of how Aki had had to go deep inside his spirit after a burrowing Phantom particle.

"Yes, indeed we do," Dr. Sid said. "You see, the injured particles escape. Let me emphasis that term again. They *escape*."

As he talked, the image of the space station came back, with the Zeus beam again being fired at the crater. Only this time the image followed the beam down into the crater, showing the meteor being destroyed. But not all the Phantoms.

"They bury or dig themselves deeper into a patient's body," Dr. Sid said. "And when we increase the laser power to destroy those deeper particles, we have had incidents resulting in further injury to the patient and, in some cases, death."

On the screen, the image showed the Zeus beam cutting through the meteor and deep into the Earth, hitting and damaging a blue layer deep inside the crust.

Gray felt himself shudder. He had been very lucky yesterday. Lucky that Aki was there, and that she was as good as she was at operating on Phantom infestations.

"And what exactly do these images mean, Doctor?" Councilman Drake asked from the far end of the platform. "I'm not really following you."

Gray knew Drake was solidly behind General Hein.

"It means," Dr. Sid replied, "that there is a very good chance the beam from the Zeus cannon will burn the Phantoms in the meteor."

"Exactly," General Hein said loudly, without standing. "Thank you."

"However," Dr. Sid continued, "it also means that the beam's energy may be too strong, injuring the Earth as well."

"Injure the Earth?" Councilman Drake asked.

Dr. Sid only nodded.

"You mean the spirit of the Earth, don't you, Doctor?" Drake demanded, his voice cold and low.

Around the chamber the audience stirred and filled the air with a low murmur of talking. Gray felt uncomfortable for Dr. Sid and Aki.

"Yes," Dr. Sid said, his shoulders back as he faced the Council. "Yes, I mean the spirit of the Earth."

It was as if someone had dropped a bomb into the middle of the council chamber. Everyone seemed to be talking at once.

Gray just sat and stared at Aki. She was whispering something to Dr. Sid, who said something in return and then turned back to face the Council.

In front of Gray, General Hein stood. "This is ridiculous! How stupid do you think we are?"

His voice echoed over the chamber as the talking subsided to an uneasy silence.

After a moment General Hein went on. "Doctor, with all due respect, did you come here just to talk about some Gaia theory?"

Gray looked at Aki, who kept her gaze down. She had talked to him about Gaia. She and Dr. Sid and many others believed that everything on this planet—every plant, animal, and human spirit—came from the great spirit of the planet Earth they called Gaia. Gray had had a difficult time believing her theory, but she had told him that was all right. Given enough time, she had said she would prove it to him.

A week later she had left him.

Before Dr. Sid could respond, General Hein kept talking. "Are you trying to tell us that our planet is alive? That Earth has a spirit?" General Hein laughed. "That's a fairy tale, Doctor, and I'm sorry, but we don't have time for that."

Dr. Sid stood his ground, his back straight, facing the council. "It is not a fairy tale. It is true."

"Ah," General Hein said, taking his hands and putting them together to form the image of a gun. He pointed his hands downward. "So if I point a gun at the Earth and fire, I'm not just making a hole in the ground, but I'm killing the planet?"

Laughter broke out throughout the chamber. The sound was like a slap to Doctor Sid, but Gray watched as he stood his ground. Gray had to admit, the old guy was strong and knew his mind.

Councilwoman Hee banged her gavel, bringing the chamber to order. When she could finally be heard, she said, "Doctor Sid, the Gaia theory has not been proven."

"Even if Gaia does exist," Councilman Drake asked, "won't we still have to remove the Phantoms?"

"Yes, we will," Dr. Sid answered.

"Then," Councilman Drake said, "I think that if there is any chance of success, we should take it. Don't you agree, Doctor? Much as we do with any patient?"

"Of course I do," Dr. Sid said.

"So you agree we should use the Zeus Cannon?" General Hein asked, his words carrying to the back corners of the chamber.

"No!" the doctor said. "Not yet. I think there is an alternative to the Zeus space cannon that we must try first."

"Another method? Another weapon?" Councilwoman Hee asked as again the audience noise increased, then hushed, waiting for Dr. Sid's answer.

"Yes, a means of disabling the Phantoms."

"Please," Councilman Drake said. "Explain this to us."

General Hein dropped back into his seat with disgust.

Dr. Sid nodded, then keyed a new holographic image to take the place of the meteor crater in the middle of the chamber. This new image was of an alien spirit, swirling in sharp, red tones. Gray knew exactly what he was looking at, because Aki had shown it to him.

The audience gasped and many sat back, as if just the image of the Phantom spirit could hurt them.

Dr. Sid pointed at the image floating in the middle of the council chamber. "All the aliens display a distinct energy pattern," Dr. Sid explained. "Now it is a *fact* that two opposing bio-etheric waves, placed one over the other, will cancel each other out."

General Hein jumped to his feet as Dr. Sid went on.

"It is theoretically possible to construct a wave pattern in direct opposition to the Phantom energy."

Beside the red energy pattern, a blue one appeared, very similar.

"The operative word there is theoretically," General Hein said as the blue pattern started to match and move closer to the red pattern in the air. Gray was amazed at the idea of it all. Would it actually be possible to destroy the Phantoms simply by canceling them off the planet? After all the ones he had killed, that was hard to believe.

"We have been collecting energy signatures for that very purpose from a variety of sources," Dr. Sid said, ignoring General Hein, "including animals and plants."

Gray suddenly understood why Aki had said the weed she had gotten yesterday was worth all their lives. If Dr. Sid was right, it was.

"Doctor!" General Hein shouted over the audience noise as the two colored patterns started to merge in the air.

"We are currently assembling such a wave, and are nearing completion."

As the blue wave covered and merged with the red one, both vanished.

The audience again burst into loud talking. Gray had to admit that the images Dr. Sid had put together were compelling. But the question was, would they be enough to buy Dr. Sid and Aki some time?

Councilwoman Hee banged for order, and slowly the talking dimmed.

"Members of the Council," General Hein said, his voice holding the power of someone used to having his words listened to, "gathering plants and animals from around the world to fight the Phantoms is utter nonsense."

Put that way, Gray had to agree. It sounded stupid. The audience agreed with their snickers and laughs. Clearly this was not going well for Aki and Dr. Sid.

General Hein went on. "The Zeus space cannon is a proven, effective weapon. It will kill Phantoms. I ask you, can we afford to wait for some crazy invention, some army of touchy-feely plants and animals?"

Gray was impressed. Right now the general clearly had the audience and the Council right where he wanted them.

"Dr. Sid," General Hein said, pointing at Sid and Aki, "offers no solid evidence that his idea will destroy the aliens."

Aki jumped up from her chair. "There *is* evidence!" she shouted.

Dr. Sid tried to stop her, but she brushed him aside. Gray had no idea what she was about to do, but he had no doubt it was going to be dramatic. Aki never did anything halfway.

General Hein stood, staring at her, as if his look could cut her down.

"What is your evidence, Doctor?" Councilwoman Hee asked Aki.

Aki stared at her. "Members of the Council," Aki said. She then took a deep breath before going on.

"Our partially completed energy wave has successfully stopped Phantom particles from spreading through a terminally infected patient."

A stunned silence filled the hall as everyone took in what Aki was saying. Gray was stunned as well. Before now the only way to save a person infected with Phantom particles, as Gray had been the day before, was to destroy those particles quickly.

Suddenly the stunned silence broke once more into loud talking, as Councilwoman Hee again banged for silence.

"Doctor," Councilman Drake said to Aki, staring at her, "do you claim to have evidence that a terminal patient has been cured?"

"Not cured," Aki said. "The wave, as Dr. Sid reported, is not yet complete. But we have succeeded in containing the particles safely inside the patient by using the wave as a shield the particles cannot pass through."

Now everyone was talking, and Councilwoman Hee was making no effort to contain it. Aki just stood and stared straight ahead.

Again Gray was shocked, as was everyone else. His entire life he had lived with the fear that a single brush with a Phantom particle would bring on death if not caught and acted on quickly. Now Aki was telling him that might not be the case. It was world-altering news. It meant suddenly that the enemy he faced wasn't quite as dangerous as a moment before.

General Hein shouted over the commotion, bringing silence with the power of his command voice.

"Doctor," Hein shouted. "Where is this proof you claim to have?"

"Right here," Aki said.

She opened her tunic to show her chest covered by what looked to Gray to be a metallic wrapping of some sort. It was shiny and had a few small readout meters just above her belt

"I'm the patient," Aki said.

The council chamber was stunned into complete silence.

Aki stepped up to the holographic display, adjusted a few controls, then tapped something on the metal wrapped around her chest.

Suddenly, in the middle of the council chamber, a grotesque red shape writhed and twisted. Gray knew what it was instantly, as did everyone in the room.

Phantom particles.

"This is what is being contained inside me," Aki said. "General, I am your proof, because I am standing here talking to you, very much alive."

All Gray could do was stare in shock at the red, twisting mass of alien particles that lived inside the woman he loved.

chapter 6

The sounds of the council audience talking loudly and Councilwoman Hee hammering for order followed Aki and Dr. Sid out into the wide, white-painted hallway. Aki could feel her heart pounding and the sweat dripping off her neck. Dr. Sid was walking quickly, clearly not happy with what she had done. But Aki knew she had done the right thing. She was sure of it. General Hein couldn't be allowed to fire that weapon of his. It might destroy everything they were fighting to save.

"Dr. Sid," Aki said, "wait a moment."

Dr. Sid stopped suddenly and turned to face her. "You may have bought us some time, but I wonder at what cost. Do you know the answer to that?"

He was as angry as she had ever seen him in the years they had worked together. But now wasn't the time for her to back down. "No, I don't," she said. "But,

Doctor, I can't keep hiding in the background while you protect me."

"Dropping into old New York isn't what I call hiding," Dr. Sid replied.

Aki wasn't going to let him go that easily. She had been right and she knew it. "At some point we both knew that what happened to me, and what you did to save me was going to have to come out."

"In front of the entire Council and the world?" Dr. Sid just shook his head. "I can think of a better way of doing it."

"But not for something as important," she said. "Look, I want what life I have left to mean something." She stared at him, keeping her gaze locked with his. "Is that so hard to understand?"

"No, it's not," he said. "And when we find the seventh and eighth spirits—"

"*If* we find them," Aki said. She knew what it was going to take as well as he did. "What we need now is some luck."

Dr. Sid shook his head. "Luck has nothing to do with it. Faith and hard work is what we need, because I'll be damned if you're going to die before me. So let's get back to work."

With that he turned and walked quickly away down the corridor.

Aki stood and watched her mentor go, giving him the space he clearly wanted and needed. Maybe she had bought them some time. The Council would decide at some point, after a lot of arguing and shouting, she was sure. But at least now she didn't have to go slinking around, hiding.

And Gray knew her secret as well. She had no idea what he was thinking. She just hoped he didn't hate her.

Or worse yet, was disgusted by her.

She followed after Dr. Sid, heading for the lab. If she was going to start the search for the seventh and eighth spirits, she had a lot of work to do to get ready. And the sooner she found those spirits, the sooner she would be out of the metal that encased her chest and kept the alien within.

And the sooner she could have a real life again. If that was ever going to be possible.

The barrier that covered the city was huge, protecting an entire valley and the city below from any invasion of the Phantoms. One-hundred-story towers shot into the sky, forming lines of posts that held the bio-etheric transmitters high in the air. Each transmitter sprayed out its energy in an umbrella shape that merged with the energy from the other towers to form the barrier. The entire barrier glowed a faint orange, making the city seem as if it was always in an eternal twilight under its protective shield.

Gondola lines had been strung between the towers during the construction of the city so maintenance workers could build and service the energy transmitters without having to climb up and down each massive tower. In one single gondola she could work her way over all of the area under the barrier.

Aki had now filled one of the large service gondolas with her scanning equipment. After the council meeting, she and Dr. Sid had figured out the exact pattern of the seventh spirit. She had decided that she might as well start her search for it close to home and work outward. A night in a service gondola would allow her to scan the entire city and all its human, animal, and plant life.

It was going to be a very long night.

"The Council decided to postpone firing the Zeus cannon," Gray said from the doorway of the gondola.

Aki felt her heart race, but somehow she managed to not start and just keep adjusting the sensor equipment in front of her. "I guess I put on quite a show."

Gray came in, his weight moving the gondola slightly. He moved around, looking over the instruments filling the outer walls of the car. All the sensors lead to one machine that she pretty much needed to tend one hundred percent of the time while the scanning was going on. The seventh spirit would show up for only a few seconds, as a green dot on the monitor, and she didn't dare miss it.

He moved over to a point behind her. She could feel his presence, smell him, feel the heat from his body. She very much wanted to turn and look him in the eye, to see how he was feeling with her secret. But instead she kept working, adjusting, getting everything ready.

After a moment Gray said, "Mind if I tag along on your expedition?"

Aki turned and looked him in the eye. Clearly he wasn't mad or disgusted. She was very much relieved to see that, but she couldn't afford to let those emotions show. "You'll probably get bored."

"I'll take my chances," he said, leaning against the support post in the center of the gondola.

"Fine by me then," she said.

He said nothing more and neither did she as she finished her last-minute adjustments, made sure all the sensors were working. Then she moved around him and closed the door of the car.

The gondola shook slightly as it bumped from its station and moved out of the small building housing it. Suddenly it was hundreds of feet in the air and the sensors were feeding information to the main monitor. She pulled up her chair in front of the monitor and sat.

Gray moved over closer to try to look over her shoulder. "So what are you doing?"

He was so close behind her that they almost touched. She desperately wanted to just let him hold her again, as he used to do. Instead she said nothing.

"Oh, I see; you're giving me the silent treatment. You're right, this will get boring."

She shook her head. It was clear he wasn't going to just let things go. And a large part of her was very glad for that. "I'm scanning the city for the seventh spirit."

"The sixth was the plant yesterday?" he asked.

"Yes." She pointed at the screen in front of her. "All of these sensors patch into this monitor. If it's down there anywhere, it will show up on here."

Gray leaned past her and looked at the monitor. "So you stare at the monitor all night looking for the exact right animal, human, or plant?"

"All night," she said. "Or as long as it takes me to cover the city under the barrier."

"Sounds like a long night," he said, moving back and leaning against the gondola's center pole again.

She said nothing, and neither did he. And for the moment, that was just fine with her. She was just glad he was there with her.

chapter 7

Jane walked up behind the other two members of the Deep Eyes squad. Ryan had a scanner in his hand and had it pointed at a maintenance gondola moving slowly away from the docking area. Neil was working at the wiring on one of the control panels for the maintenance gondolas.

The darkness and the fact that their attention was focused outward allowed her to move right up on them. It wasn't often anyone could sneak up on those two.

"Hurry up, Neil," Ryan said.

"Relax, Sarge," Neil said. "I almost got it."

"Just what do you think you are doing?" Jane asked right in Neil's ear.

To his credit he didn't jump.

"You could kill a guy sneaking up on him like that," he said, looking back at her.

"I'm considering it anyway," Jane said. "So what exactly are you two doing?" These two couldn't be left alone for a minute without getting into some kind of trouble.

Ryan held out the scanner for her to look at. In it, she could see the images of two human spirits inside the maintenance gondola overhead. Nothing at all unusual.

"Who's that?" Jane asked.

"The captain and that doctor lady we pulled out of the old city."

"We're just gonna strand them for a while," Neil said.

"You're what?" Jane asked, looking at Neil as if he had lost his mind, which she was sure he had.

"Hey, don't look at me," Ryan said. "It was his idea."

"This was your idea?" she asked, turning to Neil.

"Just helping the captain out a little," Neil said, giving her his boyish smile. "Where's your sense of romance? Has it been too long and you've lost it?"

She glared at Neil and he just smiled at her. At that moment she actually thought about just beating the crap out of him and leaving. Then the feeling passed.

"You've seen how the captain looks at her," Ryan added.

Jane had to admit she had seen that. And maybe giving them a little time together wouldn't be that bad an idea after all.

A few sparks flew from the control panel and out over the city the gondola came to a swinging halt.

"Okay," Jane said. "Lets get out of here as soon as one of you puts in a call to maintenance for them to fix this."

"How about we call in ten minutes?" Ryan said, laughing. "That ought to give them enough time."

"For you, maybe," Neil said. "But if it was me up there, you'd need at least an hour."

"In your dreams," Ryan said.

"Ten minutes then," Jane said, shaking her head. "You two are crazy, you know that?"

Neil winked at her as he closed the panel. "It's *amore*, baby."

The gondola suddenly stopped, swinging back and forth before coming to rest, hanging in the air over the city. Aki glanced around, but Gray hadn't left his position against the middle pole of the car. He seemed as surprised by the sudden stop as she was.

She checked to make sure her screen was clear, then moved to the controls of the gondola. "What do you think happened?" Aki asked as she checked over the controls and found nothing that would help.

"More than likely just a glitch," Gray said. "They have automatic teams that respond any time one of these cars is stopped between stations. They should have it up and running soon enough."

Aki nodded, then went back and checked her monitor. Since they weren't moving, there was no need to keep staring at it. And if he was right about the automatic teams, there was no point in calling anyone just yet.

"Listen, Aki," Gray said. "I—"

"I'm still mad at you," Aki said, interrupting him before he could go any further. If she was going to have this talk with Gray, she was going to take the offensive.

"You're mad at *me?*" Gray asked, clearly surprised.

"Leaving your helmet on in the transport yesterday," Aki said. "Not telling me who you were. Doesn't that seem a little *childish* to you?"

"Well," Gray said, shaking his head, "I was just a little upset when you packed up and left without saying a word. And not answering my calls is a little more than childish I would say."

Aki turned and looked out the window at the barrier-covered city below. It was a beautiful sight, but tonight she didn't much care about the beauty.

"Well, now you know what was going on," she said after a moment of silence.

"Yeah," Gray said, "now I know."

"So, I'm *sorry*," Aki said. And she truly was. She had wanted to tell Gray. She had thought about it a number of times, and come close to calling him at least twice, but Dr. Sid had sworn her to complete secrecy. Until today, she couldn't make herself break that promise. Not even to Gray.

"Well," Gray said, "me, too. So we're both sorry."

Silence again filled the gondola. A very uneasy silence that Aki had no idea how to break.

"So," Gray said, "would you tell me about them?"

"About what?" Aki asked, looking into his eyes for the first time in a long while. She could see real caring and love and concern still in those eyes. And that relaxed her. He wasn't disgusted by the alien particles trapped inside her.

"About the spirits you've collected," Gray said.

Aki nodded. She took a deep breath, trying to figure out where to even begin. It had all happened so fast, yet the beginning seemed a lifetime ago.

"I was infected by a Phantom during an experiment. Normally, with my type of infection, no one would have survived."

"The last day I saw you?"

She nodded.

Gray stayed where he was against the pole, but she could tell he really cared. "How *did* you survive?"

"Dr. Sid," Aki said, remembering that day—as if she could ever forget those events. The moment she had gotten infected, she had thought she was as good as dead. But Dr. Sid wouldn't hear it. He had moved faster than she had believed possible.

"How?" Gray asked. "What did he do?"

Aki shrugged. "Technical stuff, mostly. In essence, he created a membrane around the infection, keeping me alive and the infection trapped. It worked, and we discovered right then that the first spirit wave was me."

"You?" Gray asked.

Aki nodded. "My spirit forms part of the wave that is the opposite of a Phantom spirit wave. It is the only reason I am alive today. It was enough to trap the Phantom particles and keep them from immediately spreading and killing me."

Gray nodded.

"The second spirit was a fish. We got lucky and found it almost at once."

"A fish?" Gray asked.

Aki nodded. She had had trouble believing it at first also, but it had been a fish. "Its wave added to mine made the shield inside me even stronger. Each spirit we find controls the Phantom particles and makes my shield more secure."

Gray nodded, clearly understanding what she was saying, so she went on. "The third spirit was a deer I found in a wildlife preserve outside Moscow. The fourth, a bird."

Gray shook his head. "How did you ever find them?"

"It wasn't easy," Aki said, laughing. "Ever try to track a sparrow from outer space? It's no fun." She looked into his eyes and then laughed. "What am I saying? You probably would love that."

Gray laughed, and even more of the tension filling the stalled gondola eased. "You're right, I probably would."

"And then there was that plant I collected in the old city," she said.

"I thought that was number six?" Gray asked.

Aki had hoped he wouldn't catch that.

"You skipped one," Gray said. "What was number five?"

Aki sighed and stared at the nonmoving images on the monitor. "The fifth was a little girl, dying in a hospital emergency room."

"You're not kidding, are you?" Gray asked.

She shook her head and stared at the empty screen as she talked. "I told her everything had a spirit. Dogs, cats, trees, little girls, even the Earth. I told her that she wasn't dying, just returning to Earth's spirit, Gaia."

The silence again filled the gondola as Gray waited for Aki to finish. She could remember that day so vividly. Just thinking about it brought tears to her eyes. She glanced up at Gray. The concern in his eyes touched her. He did care about what she was going through, what she had felt, so she finished the story.

"That little girl told me that she was ready to die and that I didn't need to make up stories to make her feel better."

Aki took a deep breath. "Imagine, only seven years old and ready to die."

Gray moved over beside her and put his hand on her shoulder. It felt wonderful, but it wasn't what she needed at that moment. What she needed was to get the stupid gondola moving again so she could find the other two spirits.

"I'm sorry," Gray said.

She turned away from his touch and studied her still blank and unmoving screen. "I have work to do."

Gray stayed behind her, his very presence both confusing and comforting her at the same time. Finally she couldn't pretend to look at the monitor any more. She turned and looked up into his eyes.

"You don't really believe any of this, do you?"

Gray shrugged, but didn't turn away. "You're asking me if I believe that all life, even the planet Earth itself, has a living spirit?"

"I am," she said.

"And that we are all born from, and when we die we return to, this Gaia?"

She nodded.

"Honestly," Gray said, "I just don't know."

An honest answer. She would have seen through anything else and he knew it.

He reached out and pulled her toward him.

She let him hold her, not relaxing into him as she wanted to do, but enjoying the warmth of him.

He traced the top of her metal shield just under her

shoulder, then ran his finger up her neck, sending shivers down her spine. His touch was always so gentle, so wonderful. Why hadn't she let him remain part of her life?

"You could have told me, you know," he said, his words seeming to come from her mind, their intent soft and without even a hint of anger.

"I know," she said, relaxing into his arms even more. "But I just don't know how long I have left."

"Who does?" he asked.

He moved to kiss her, and she was going to let him. No, she *wanted* him to kiss her more than anything. She wanted to be held and to be told that everything would be all right.

But at that moment the gondola jerked into motion.

Aki pulled away, looked up into the eyes of the man she loved, and then turned back to her now-moving monitor. "I had better get back to scanning."

"I understand," Gray said.

He moved over and sat on one of the benches near the door. And that was where he stayed, keeping her company and giving his silent support, until she had finished her work six hours later.

chapter 8

One full day after his time in the gondola with Aki, Gray was summoned into Major Elliot's office. Elliot was the commander of the local area, reporting only to General Hein. The major's office was a comfortable room that overlooked the city. The light from the barrier filled the office with a faint orange tint that seemed almost soothing.

In the last day Gray hadn't heard anything from Aki, but hadn't expected to. She had told him she was going to be working day and night until the other two spirits were found. Even though he wanted to help her, and be with her, he knew that the best thing he could do now was let her work and stay out of her way, just as he had done during the time in the gondola.

Gray knew Major Elliot pretty well, since they had both come up through the ranks at about the same time. He didn't much care for Elliot, since he was a "yes-man" to General Hein. Usually being summoned to the major's office was nothing more than a social visit to try to gain support for some cause the general was pushing, but Gray could tell from the major's posture as he stood behind his desk this was not one of those times.

It took Gray a moment to realize that he and Major Elliot were not the only ones in the room. General Hein was standing near the window, looking over the city, his back to the door. Clearly something was happening, and Gray guessed that he and Deep Eyes were to be a part of it.

He saluted and Major Elliot returned his salute, but didn't offer him a seat. There was no doubt this was very official and very important.

"Captain Edwards," the major said, "you and Deep Eyes extracted a Dr. Aki Ross from old New York several days ago, did you not?"

"Yes, sir," Gray said, stunned at the mention of Aki's name. But he should have know this would be about her. After what she had done in the council chamber and to General Hein, how could it *not* be about her?

"And she saved your life from a Phantom infestation, did she not?"

"Yes, sir, she did."

General Hein did not move from his position at the window. It was almost as if he wasn't listening, but Gray knew better than that. The general missed very little.

"What were your impressions of Dr. Ross that day?" the major asked.

Gray had no idea just how much they knew about his relationship with Aki, so he answered the question as it was posed. "She seemed very capable and determined, sir. She got what she went in for and we helped her get out."

Major Elliot nodded, then looked down at his desk for a moment before looking Gray in the eyes. "You and Deep Eyes are being temporarily reassigned. You will guard Dr. Ross when she reenters the wasteland."

Gray was even more shocked now. Aki, in the last day, must have found the location of the seventh spirit, but what could be alive in the wasteland?

"Understood, sir," Gray said, keeping his thoughts and emotions hidden.

"No," General Hein said from his place near the window, "you don't understand yet, Captain."

General Hein turned and looked at Gray. The general's gaze felt like lasers cutting through him. Gray returned the stare, waiting for the general to explain.

"You are to report any aberrant behavior in Dr. Ross to Major Elliot immediately."

" 'Aberrant behavior,' sir?" Gray asked, wanting to make sure he was very clear on what the general meant.

General Hein looked back out at the city. "The woman carries an alien infestation, Captain."

Gray said nothing. The general knew he had been at the council meeting when Aki did her show-and-tell bit to buy time for her and Dr. Sid's project.

"We don't know what it may be doing to her," General Hein said, turning to again look at Gray.

Gray said nothing, so the general went on. "The alien presence could be affecting her judgement. For all we know, they may be manipulating the doctor for their very own purposes."

"Is the general suggesting that Dr. Ross is a spy?" Gray asked. He didn't like at all what Hein was saying about Aki. There was no way the woman he had spent the night with in the gondola was any type of spy.

General Hein laughed. "The general is wondering why he's explaining himself to a captain."

Gray said nothing, let nothing show on his face.

General Hein stared at him, his gaze piercing.

"She's had prolonged exposure to Phantom tissue," Major Elliot said, moving to break the tension. "If this begins to manifest itself in any way, Dr. Ross is to be placed under arrest and transported for observation. Do I make myself very clear, *Captain?*"

"Perfectly, sir," Gray said.

Hein laughed, then said. "It is, in fact, for her own good. You should know that, Captain."

"Of course, sir," Gray said. But he didn't believe a word of it, and he had no doubt that the general thought he did.

Major Elliot saluted him and Gray returned the salute, then turned and headed for the door. He had no doubt at all that, after that exchange, some of the general's hand-picked men would be going along wherever he, Aki, and Deep Eyes went.

He pulled the door closed behind him, staring down the hallway. There was also no doubt that he and Deep Eyes were just pawns in a plan to somehow get Aki and Dr. Sid out of General Hein's way.

If Gray had anything to say about it, that wouldn't happen.

chapter 9

They came on like a wind from the center of hell.

Aki stood her ground as the Earth trembled around her, more real in her dream than it should be.

Then another rumbling was added to the first, just as it had been other nights, and lately every time she tried to even nap.

The very air seemed as if it might shake into nothingness. She turned to see a second alien army hurling itself at the first army.

She stood in the middle, in the way of the two hordes of alien creatures carrying strange weapons, their armor shining in the hot sun.

They were attacking each other, destroying this land and each other.

The screaming and shouting and fighting sounds increased until it hurt her ears. She held her head, trying to block the sound, but the noise only increased as the two armies swarmed closer and closer.

Then, just at the moment Aki usually woke up, the two armies collided in battle.

The carnage around her was beyond belief. They tore at each other, smashed bodies, ripped limbs and armor falling away like paper. Balls of fire mixed with lasers as the two armies fought.

She stood in the middle of it all, not touched, not believing what she was witnessing. Death seemed to flow everywhere, pounding the world she stood on.

Then, as if someone had stopped them all with a single command, the fighting ceased, and every remaining soldier in the two armies turned and looked toward her.

The silence was clear and complete, filling every ounce of her being.

Why were they looking at her?

What did they want with her?

Why was she even there?

Then, behind her, a roaring sound slowly grew until it punched through the silence like a hammer pounding on the back of her head.

She knew they weren't looking at her, but beyond her.

Something else was coming.

Something far, far worse.

She woke up before she could turn and see. She hated not knowing, hated the dreams for making her wait, hated even the thought of sleeping.

She tried to calm her racing heart and listen. Around her the transport carrying her and Deep Eyes was silent as everyone either drifted in their own thoughts or slept. In the cockpit, Neil was flying.

Outside the window beside her she could see an area of the central part of what had been the United States. The ground was dead and brown. Life in this area had vanished long ago.

She glanced at the time, then took a deep, shuddering breath and let it out slowly, making sure no one else on the transport noticed her. She had been asleep for less than ten minutes. There was no way she was going to try to go back to sleep again, even though she should rest. Not after watching those alien armies slaughter each other like that.

Dream or no dream, that had *felt* real.

She sighed. She was now convinced that these dreams were some form of communication from the Phantoms.

She shifted in her seat and looked around. She couldn't believe she had even thought that. If General Hein knew what she was thinking, she'd be locked up so fast and so deep, no one would ever find her.

Dr. Sid's words about destroying everything were clear in her mind. She glanced behind her. Gray was leaning against one bulkhead, his eyes closed. Jane was reading something. General Hein's three men were in their armor, and she had no idea what they were doing or even thinking. She didn't much like the idea that they were even on this mission, but after what she had done in the Council, it made sense that the general would want his people watching her.

She let one hand rub against the vest she wore. She knew that the Phantoms inside her were beginning to win. She just hoped she had enough energy and time to get the last two spirits before they did.

She leaned back in her seat and stared out the window. Dr. Sid was right. For the moment, until things changed completely, her dreams might not be her own, but her thoughts were still hers. And right now, she would keep those thoughts to herself.

For Aki, the next twenty minutes went slowly as she sat watching the landscape flash past under the transport. Everything below them was now looking more and more like the images in her dreams. Aki knew it wasn't the same, but the fact that humans fighting Phantoms had turned parts of Earth into a wasteland, just as the alien armies of her dreams had turned another place into the same thing, bothered her a lot.

Below her the dead surface was pockmarked with bomb craters. Twisted hunks of metal were all that was left of vehicles. Tree trunks had been smashed off at ground level in the long-ago battle for this area. Clearly the humans had lost. And the carnage seemed to go on forever.

Aki had been stunned when the reconnaissance from orbit found the seventh spirit in this old battleground. So had Dr. Sid. There hadn't been a sign of life in this area for twenty years. Nothing could live out here with the Phantoms, yet there was the signal tracking the energy of the seventh spirit, right in the middle of this desolation.

Aki watched a vast area littered with the remains of human soldiers flash past below, then turned away. Around her the transport was silent.

Gray and the Deep Eyes were in their armor, with their helmets stored under their seats. Neil was flying the transport while Jane studied a holographic image of the terrain, using Aki's data to track where they were headed. The seventh spirit was a green blinking dot on the screen, calling to them.

General Hein's three men had still not taken off any of their full armor, leaving even their helmets in place. Dr. Sid had warned her that her revelation to the Council would not sit well with the military. She would be considered a traitor to humans the moment she did something wrong, just because there was an alien trapped inside her. And those three were with this mission to make sure her first mistake would be her last.

So she wasn't going to do anything wrong, just let the general stew until they found the last two spirits and solved all this. Then he could take his Zeus Cannon and shove it.

To the left of the transport Aki could see the few tall buildings still standing in old Tucson.

"Our target is fifty klicks west of the old Tucson barrier city," Jane said.

Aki knew there was nothing left there either. The battle they were flying over had been the last stand for this entire area.

"Roger," Neil replied from the cockpit.

"Phantom concentration?" Gray asked.

Jane looked over at her captain with a very sick frown. Then she shook her head and went back to monitoring her holo-panel. Aki saw the look and knew, without Jane saying anything, that there were a vast number of Phantoms in this area. Large Phantoms, from what she understood. The biggest on the planet.

"Exactly what are you reading?" one of General

Hein's men asked, his voice firm and cold. Aki didn't like any of the three, and hadn't even bothered to try to get their names, even if they would have given them to her.

"Not good," Jane said. "We've got big metas every- where."

Meta Phantoms, as Jane called them, were known to grow the size of battleships, and regular weapons didn't stop them without exact hits. They could reach out with their tentacles and cover the space of a dozen city blocks. And one swipe from one of their tentacles killed instantly. Some of them could even fly. Aki knew that the Phantoms she had gone up against in old New York were nothing compared to these.

"So it's gonna be a real picnic," Ryan said.

"Basic fire is going to be ineffective," Gray said. "Build up your charges and make them count."

He turned and looked at her, giving her a half smile. "Stick close to me," he said. "No heroics today?"

She nodded.

"Everything by the book," he said, his gaze not leav- ing hers.

"By the book," she said, smiling at him. "Right."

And this time she meant it. Tangling with a Meta Phantom was not something she ever wanted to do. She didn't even want to see one up close. Pictures had been more than enough.

Jane brought up a rough map of their destination on a holographic image floating in front of Gray. "We can drop energy buoys here, here, and here." Red lights ap- peared on the screen as she talked.

Aki noticed that the red lights indicating the energy

buoys surrounded the blinking green of the spirit they were after.

Gray nodded. "That should allow us time to land and get the target."

"And with luck," Jane said, "get out before the Phantoms even know we are there."

"The idea being that the buoys will attract the Phantoms, right?" Aki asked. She understood how Phantom energy and particles affected humans, and that Phantoms were attracted by certain types of energy, but she knew little of how the military used that information.

"Yeah," Jane said, her voice not very convincing.

There was silence around the transport. Aki looked into Gray's eyes. He wasn't looking any more convincing than Jane sounded.

"For a while," Gray said. "We're going to have to be quick with this."

The tension in the transport made the air feel thick and heavy to Aki. She hadn't been this worried about any of her spirit retrieval missions, including dropping into old New York.

Finally Ryan broke the silence. He turned to General Hein's men. "So, you're from the 307s? Ever done any wasteland re-con before?"

The three said nothing. Not even their gazes altered.

Ryan shrugged and turned away. "It can get pretty ugly."

Again the heavy tension of silence settled over the transport. Below, the wasteland flashed past, filled with the dead of a long-ago battle that had turned the war with the Phantoms against the humans. Aki knew her history well enough to know that, after this major battle, humans had retreated behind the barriers, venturing out only to keep the Phantoms at bay.

The only good thing since this battle had been humanity managing to get back into space and build the space stations and the Zeus cannon weapon station. Even though the Phantoms had come from space on the asteroid, it seemed they couldn't get back into space. And the humans were starting to use that advantage more and more. Aki knew it was the only advantage they had.

"Buoy away," Jane said.

"Hang on!" Neil shouted as he banked the transport hard to the right, forcing Aki to grab onto the wall to keep from sliding back into Gray.

The transport skimmed over the rough ground until Jane said again, "Buoy away."

Again Neil turned the transport hard right and after a moment Jane said, "Last buoy in position, Captain."

Neil once again yanked the transport hard to the right, into a position in the middle of the three buoys.

"Initiate them," Gray said. "And take us to the target. Fast."

Out the window Aki could see a bright blue light flash into being. She recognized the light instantly as coming from ovo energy cells. More than likely the cells were encased inside a small barrier glass. The light from the buoy would make the Phantoms visible to the naked human eye, as well as attract them.

Aki could see a massive Phantom appear and turn toward the energy. Then other Phantoms did the same.

Neil dropped the transport down hard and fast, into

a small open area. Out the window Aki could see they had landed in the remains of what had been a fearsome battle. As far as she could see there were rusting tanks, twisted metal, and bodies. Human bodies, still covered in their armor.

"Helmets on," Gray ordered. "Let's go, people. Neil, stay ready to pick us up."

"You got it," Neil said from the cockpit.

As the Deep Eyes stood and snapped on helmets, the transport door smashed to the ground, forming a ramp down.

Jane went out first, taking point, her weapon at ready.

Ryan was right behind her.

When Jane turned to the right, he looked left, then when her head came back left, he looked right. They were a perfectly functioning team.

Gray indicated that Aki should be at his side.

She nodded, then pulled her sensor off her hip and flipped it on as they moved down the ramp. She was the only one not in any kind of armor, and she was glad of that as the hot desert air smashed into her. The dryness of everything around her, including the air, made everything feel brittle. The air was perfectly still, and it smelled of dust and age. It had been a very long time since a live human had seen this place.

Or anything else alive, for that matter.

At the bottom of the ramp she stepped over a human body, one leg torn off, the bone white and sticking out.

Around her the Deep Eyes had spread out, taking up defensive positions.

Behind her, General Hein's three men came down the ramp.

Aki looked around, letting her sensor get a target line on the seventh spirit. They had landed on the side of a slight ridge. Below, in a shallow valley, Aki could see a swarm of Phantoms hovering around a bright blue light. They were massive, shaped like some kind of nightmare insect. It was the most horrific sight Aki had ever seen.

"Looks like they have taken the bait," Gray said softly, as if speaking too loud would attract the monsters.

No one said anything as Gray looked at her. She studied her sensor, its blinking light indicating that they were close to the spirit. It was just over the slight ridge to her right. She pointed in that direction.

Gray nodded and signaled they move out.

With Gray beside her, Aki lead, following the blinking signal of her scanner. With each step the signal got more intense.

The others spread out behind them, forming a human spear cutting slowly through the old battlefield.

Aki could not believe the number of human dead that filled this wasteland. Humanity had put up one of its biggest fights right here, and lost. And, in that loss, had given up most of the planet to the Phantoms.

She forced herself to take deep, slow breaths of the hot air to ease her nerves. The beeping of the scanner was the only thing that was important right now.

They crested the small ridge to face even more wreckage. From what Aki could tell, directly in front of them was the mixed mess of a plane and a few tanks, smashed together.

The sensor was clear now. They were close. "The seventh spirit should just be beyond that line of wreckage."

Gray nodded and headed toward a gap in the twisted metal. "I don't see how any living thing could survive out here."

"We'll find out soon enough," Aki said.

Carefully they worked their way through and over the rough ground, wrecked equipment, and human remains. The carnage around them seemed to be endless. Not even in her nightmare had she seen death like this.

At one point they came upon what looked to be the remains of a massive ovo-pac, similar to the buoys they had dropped, only antique-looking.

"This area was the first part of the overall battle," Ryan said, his voice low and controlled. "It all started out as a Phantom cleansing mission. My father is in here somewhere."

Aki jerked, then looked around at the twisted remains of humans that littered the ground like rocks. There was nothing any of them could say. She couldn't imagine how Ryan was managing this, stepping over bodies, any one of which might be his father.

Jane turned to look at Ryan, then nodded in support.

Aki looked back to her sensor. The seventh spirit was close. Very close.

Suddenly something else moved on her monitor. She looked around, then glanced up. A beautiful hawk glided effortlessly on the hot updrafts.

"I'll be damned," Ryan said.

"A survivor," Aki said.

"What's it doing out here?" Gray asked.

"Maybe hoping for life to return," Aki said.

"Is that our spirit, Doc?" Ryan asked.

"No," Aki said, checking the sensor. The seventh spirit was right in front of them, a very short distance.

Aki moved forward, forced to step on a fallen soldier, his arm forever reaching for something in front of him. In the distance the swarm of Phantoms massed around one of the buoys, almost entirely blocking out the blue light of the ovo-pac.

The faint beeping on her sensor was now almost a continuous noise. "We're closing in on the life-form we need."

"Distance?" Gray asked.

"Hard to say," Aki said, moving the scanner from side to side. "We're very close. It should be right in front of us."

"I don't see anything," Gray said.

In front of them was another body of a solider lying facedown in the dirt. As she passed the body, the readings on her sensor reversed, as if she was now moving away from the spirit.

She stopped and turned around. Everything on her scanner said it was right in front of her, but the only thing there was the body of the soldier. That couldn't be.

Gray stopped beside her and looked at where she was aiming the scanner. "You're not going to tell me it's him?"

Aki just kept studying the scanner, moving it down closer and closer to the body of the long-dead soldier.

"That's impossible," Ryan said.

"Yeah," Jane said.

"Defensive positions, people," Gray ordered.

He pointed out where he wanted the three general's men as well. They formed an outward-facing circle around her and Gray.

He looked at her and she nodded. It had to be the place. Something was alive here. Something was the seventh spirit. But what could it be?

Gray reached down and rolled over the body of the soldier.

A white skull was visible through the faceplate of the helmet. Parts of the skeleton fell free as the armor broke apart, exposing bones and old clothes.

Aki's scanner still told her the spirit was there. She took the eye-scope out of the side of the scanner and put it over her right eye, adjusting it quickly. She had set the eye-scope to show her exactly the shape and size of the spirit. As she put it on, it became clear what she had been looking for. The seventh spirit was the dead soldier's portable ovo-pack, used to power his weapon so long ago.

The idea froze her for a moment. She took a deep breath and bent down, studying the old hardware.

"It's not the soldier or a plant under him," Aki said. "It's his ovo-pack."

"What?" Ryan said, glancing back for a moment before turning to keep up his watch.

"How can that be?" Gray asked. "The ovo-packs power our weapons, the barrier cities, everything we use against the Phantoms. It's just bio-etheric energy."

"And to create that energy," Aki said, "we use living tissue. Single-cell organisms."

"You're telling me his backpack is the seventh spirit?" Gray asked.

"Yes," she said, getting it loose enough to pick up.

"We have incoming," Neil said, his voice clear over the com link from the ship.

Aki stood as Gray glanced around.

"This side, too," Jane said.

"And here," Ryan said.

Aki could see that suddenly the Phantoms were all around them, coming in over the rocks and wreckage, their shapes illuminated by the energy from the ovopacks they had dropped. They were all massive. One seemed to tower into the sky like a building, moving slowly. Others resembled giant kites, twisting and looping in midair; others were like sea serpents diving into water, with tails spanning hundreds of meters.

Suddenly one of General Hein's men was attacked by a part of one of the big kite-like Phantoms that came up out of the ground under him.

The guy screamed, the sound echoing over the hot battlefield.

Aki knew instantly it was too late for him as the Phantom ripped out his spirit, releasing sparkling blue electrical energy in the process. She watched in horror as the soldier's blue spirit floated in the hot air for a moment before vanishing.

An instant later the soldier's body slumped to the ground, dead.

Jane took the Phantom out with one shot.

"Ryan," Gray shouted, "get this soldier's pack."

Aki could do nothing but watch as Ryan took the seventh spirit out of the dead soldier's backpack. The calm, quiet desert air was now cut with the sound of firing as the others opened up at the oncoming aliens.

It was an amazing sight as the Phantoms, their shapes illuminated by the light from the buoys, turned toward them. It was so frightening, she felt almost drunk. Giddy.

Her mind told her that was wrong. Yet it was how she felt, and she couldn't seem to control it.

"Those buoys?" Aki said to Gray as he fired and killed a large Phantom coming at them from the south.

"Yeah," Gray said.

"They're not working," Aki said. She giggled to herself.

"Thank you," Gray said, glancing at her.

She tried to make the smile stop, but for some reason she couldn't. This wasn't supposed to be funny. They were all in danger of being killed.

But suddenly that didn't seem to matter either.

Part of her mind shouted that something was wrong. Something was controlling her.

The other part didn't care.

Suddenly everything around Aki seemed to spin.

The world seemed to go into slow motion; the intense desert heat cut at her, making her sweat. How could Gray stand it out here with that massive armor on? He had to be cooking like a crab in a pot of boiling water.

She laughed at the thought, the sound lost in the blazing of weapon fire.

Her attention turned to the sound, and suddenly it was as if each shot was coming from inside her.

"Are you all right?" Gray asked, staring at her.

His voice sounded distant and slowed down.

"Of course I am," she said, but even to her own ears the sound of her words seemed hollow. She put her hands over her ears, but that didn't help.

"Let's get the hell out of here!" Gray shouted. "Standard formation. Jane, take point."

"Man," Jane said as she blew apart a kite Phantom. "Something's not right about this. This shouldn't be happening."

Aki stumbled over a rock as they scrambled back up the hill. It felt as if the ground was a hundred miles below her, and her legs weren't even there anymore.

Gray had her under the arm and was pulling her along. She couldn't remember when he had grabbed her. She was lucky he was here.

Maybe they could just stop for a moment and rest. Then she could tell him how lucky she was to know him. Maybe he would even let her kiss him. That would be nice.

"Something's attracting them!" Ryan shouted as he blew apart two Phantoms coming at them from over the top of the hill.

"Neil, get us out of here!" Gray shouted.

Aki could no longer even feel the earth. It was as if she was watching the events and the battle from a distance. Almost through the eyes of the Phantoms themselves.

And none of it seemed to matter to her.

"They're right on us!" Jane shouted, never slowing her fire.

Aki could see the transport thousands of miles off as

it swept toward them. Part of her knew that wasn't the case, but it seemed that way.

Oh well, it didn't matter.

She was hot.

The light was so bright.

Gray's hand hurt under her arm.

Why did they have to make so much noise?

She had to rest.

What was wrong with stopping?

Sitting down was good.

She had to stop.

The ground was her friend. The others could just go on without her. She didn't care.

She wanted to tell Gray to take the ovo-pack to Dr. Sid, but then it didn't feel important enough to even bother.

She twisted sideways and felt Gray release her. Now she was free to stop and rest.

She had to rest.

Maybe even a little nap.

She felt the distant pain of her knees hitting the dirt, then her chest and head.

She didn't care about that, either. It almost seemed funny.

The last thought she had was to wonder why resting hurt so much.

chapter 10

Gray couldn't believe it when Aki twisted away from him and fell face-first into the dirt. With a quick shot he took out a large flying Phantom coming over a wrecked tank, then bent down and flipped her over. "Aki, can you hear me?"

Nothing. Not even a flutter from her eyelids.

"Captain!" Ryan shouted, "we got to keep moving!"

He used both arms to scoop her up. She seemed heavier than she should be, and the metal wrapped around her chest and back was hard and hot to the touch. She was completely unconscious and her breathing was very shallow. She needed help and she needed it fast.

"Fire in the hole!" Jane shouted, who fired past Gray, taking out a Phantom that was coming up behind Gray.

Gray nodded his thanks to Jane. Neil had the transport hovering just in front of them, the ramp down and waiting. Gray shouted, "Make a run for it! Keep it tight, people!"

As a unit, the Deep Eyes took off, staying in diamond formation with him taking the point, carrying Aki. General Hein's two remaining men brought up the rear, running and firing behind them as best they could.

The distance to the transport wasn't far, not more than fifty meters, but the ground was rough and covered with battle debris and dead bodies. The run seemed to take forever, and with every jolt he worried about Aki, and what it was doing to her. But at the moment they just didn't have any other choice. She might live this way. Slowing down would no doubt be deadly to all of them.

Ahead, Gray could see there were Phantoms coming in at the transport from all sides. They had to clear the area around the transport, at least back far enough to give them time to get it in the air. Considering how many of the flying Phantoms were swarming at them, including some huge Metas, that wasn't going to be an easy task.

He shifted Aki to his shoulder, freeing his right arm and gun, just in time to take out a Phantom coming up from the ground ten feet ahead of them.

"Neil!" Gray shouted as they got within fifty paces of the transport. "Get ready to lift!"

"Yes, sir!" Neil said.

"The rest of you clear them back from the transport. Jane front, Ryan the rear. Thirty seconds is all we have, people."

It worked like it should. He stopped with Aki on his shoulder near the bottom of the ramp and cut down anything he could see coming on the other side of the transport, firing under the ship.

Jane went right, Ryan left, laying down fire constantly, taking out any Phantom that might be close enough to reach the transport before they could get into the air.

Gray headed up the steps and inside with Aki. He laid her out on the deck, then jumped to the tactical chair.

A few seconds later General Hein's men got in, followed by Jane and Ryan, both firing as they came up the ramp.

"Meta coming in fast!" Jane said as the hatch slammed closed.

A Meta could expand out so far that they seemed to cover entire city blocks, and they liked to come in from above, using their vast size to trap their targets under them.

"Get us out of here, Neil!" Gray shouted.

"I'd love to sir," Neil shouted as the transport lifted off the ground, clearing them from anything coming up under them, "but I got a Meta blocking—"

"Just do it!" Gray ordered as the tactical hologram came into focus, showing the Meta over them. There was an opening, but a small one. "Head right and keep it low and fast!"

The transport spun and shot off, skimming over the ridge right between two smaller Phantoms and out from under the Meta.

Gray studied the holo-image and the surrounding

landscape. There were Metas everywhere, more than he could have ever imagined in one place. And they were so big there was no chance the transport could get over them safely. They were going to have to find a way through them.

To the right a rock cliff-face was cut by a steep-walled canyon. It looked to be the least occupied by Metas, and maybe the ship could slip through there.

"Neil, see the canyon to the right?" Gray asked.

"On it, Captain," Neil said, banking the transport first to the right to go around a massive Meta coming up at them like a thundercloud boiling with energy, then back toward the opening in the rocks.

"Jane, take over here," Gray said.

He slipped out of the chair and Jane sat down.

Then he knelt beside Aki and pulled her shirt aside to look at the holo-image on her chest. The alien infestation seemed to be swarming and squirming on the screen, much harder and faster than it had done in front of the council. Clearly she was losing her fight with the Phantom particles inside her, or something had happened to her shielding in the heat.

"We have to get her to a hospital," he said to Jane at tactical. "Get Neil directions on how to get us out of this mess. And make it fast."

"You have your orders, sir," one of General Hein's men said.

Gray shook his head, not really believing what he had heard. He stood to face two drawn pistols.

The general's two men had put aside their rifles and now held standard bullet-firing pistols. They were both sitting, facing Gray, Ryan, Aki, and Jane. Neither one had taken off their helmets, so Gray could not see their faces or their eyes.

Ryan was near the cockpit. "Are you two nuts?"

"What the hell is going on here?" Gray demanded, although he knew very well what it was. General Hein had sent these men to watch him. He had been ordered to arrest Aki the moment she showed any signs of strangeness. Clearly, having that many Phantoms come after them and her passing out would qualify, under the general's orders. But at the moment that didn't much matter to him. He wasn't going to let her die in some jail cell to satisfy a power-hungry General Hein.

"Doctor Ross is to be taken into custody now, sir!" one soldier said.

"I'm sorry to interrupt your fun and games," Neil said from the cockpit, "but I'm facing a wall of Metas here. I could use a little help!"

Jane turned her attention back to the tactical holo. "Right! Up the next side canyon."

Outside of the transport the canyon walls flashed past, sometimes just inches from the transport wings.

"Lower your weapons!" Gray said, keeping his voice as low and forceful as he could. "That's an order."

One of General Hein's men shook his head. "I'm sorry, sir. We have no choice but to relieve you of your command. Please put aside your weapons."

"This woman needs medical attention," Gray said, pointing at Aki. "You can arrest her after she is treated."

"Those are not our orders," one of the general's men said. "We are to arrest her. And you. What happens after that is not our business."

"You are some cold-blooded mother," Ryan said.

"I won't let you do this, soldier," Gray said, trying to keep the anger out of his voice. "You're going to have to shoot me."

"Stand down, Captain," the man said.

Ryan moved to flank Gray. Even though Jane remained at the tactical, helping Neil weave through the Metas, her posture made it clear she was with Gray and ready to act. Three to two. Gray had no doubt the Deep Eyes would win, but someone would be hurt in the process, and he didn't want that if he could help it.

The tension filled the cabin of the transport.

And the silence, broken only by the engine sounds and the faint cussing from Neil in the cockpit.

Gray stood, braced against the transport's sudden movements, never taking his attention from the two men in front of him as Jane shouted to Neil, "Go left and over the ridge."

"Man, they are everywhere," Neil shouted back.

"I can see that," Jane said.

"So, which way?" Neil asked, the panic not far below the surface of his voice.

"No way is completely open," Jane said. "You're going to have to try to get between a couple of them."

"Oh, just great," Neil said.

Gray watched the two men pointing guns at him.

It was a stand-off inside and outside the transport.

And at his feet, the woman he loved was dying. Something needed to happen and happen fast.

He just didn't know what.

chapter 11

They came on like a wind from the center of hell.

She always thought the same thing, with every dream. It seemed to be the right image. She had become so familiar with the dream, it was as if she was observing it, not living in it.

Yet the fear was still there. She felt the fear, observed it, wondered if it was her fear, or did it belong to the Phantom particles trapped inside her.

Or maybe a little of both.

The ground under her, and the air around her, shook and rumbled. She turned to see a second alien army hurling itself at the first army.

She stood in the middle, in the way of the two hordes of alien creatures carrying strange weapons. Energy weapons. She could see that now.

Each army was completely focused on the other.

And now she could see they were not Phantoms, but

these creatures were actually alive. Only they were shaped in some of the Phantom shapes. And something about that bothered her. She just couldn't put her finger on what, exactly.

As she did every dream, she held her ears, trying to block the screaming and gunfire and the sounds of death, but the noise only increased as the two armies swarmed in battle, in and around her, fighting, yet not touching her.

She stood in the middle of it all, not believing all the anger and death, even after having this dream so many times, and in such detail.

Then, as before, the fighting suddenly ceased and every remaining soldier in the two armies turned and looked toward her.

The silence was clear and complete, filling every ounce of her being.

She knew now they were not looking at her, but beyond her. She turned to look in the same direction.

A roaring sound slowly grew until it punched through the silence like a hammer pounding on the back of her head.

Something else was coming.

And that something else was a wall of fire.

Angry colors of orange and red covered everything, stretching from the ground to the sky and as far left as she could see, to as far right.

A wall of fire was coming fast, destroying everything.

It would destroy her as well.

She knew it.

There was no escaping it.

The armies around her panicked and started to run,

but she stood her ground. She knew instinctively, in her dream-state, that there was no place to run to. It was as if she was observing something that had already happened, not something that was happening.

The wall got closer and closer, moving impossibly fast. She stared into it, trying to understand it, see what it really was. Every nerve in her body wanted her to turn and run.

Every thought said stay. This was only a dream. She needed to understand the dream.

But all she saw was a world being destroyed, completely and totally.

As the heat started to bubble and melt everything around her, she screamed—

The standoff, as far as Gray could see, wasn't going to end well. General Hein's two remaining men were trained soldiers, willing to shoot him for their mission. And Jane and Ryan were willing to die for Gray.

"Hard left!" Jane shouted. "Hole opening between two of the Metas near the line of wreckage."

"I see it," Neil said from the cockpit. His focus was completely on getting them out of the aliens and home. Gray knew Neil had no idea what was happening behind him, and it was much better that way.

Gray braced himself against the chair as the transport banked. General Hein's two men were both still seated and leaned easily into the motion.

Then, right in the middle of the turn, Aki sat up, directly facing one of Hein's men, and screamed.

To Gray it was a scream that sounded like death coming. Never had he heard such terror.

"What was that?" Neil shouted from the cockpit.

Then things happened fast.

The soldier directly facing Aki was so startled by her sudden movement and scream that he came up out of his chair and fired point blank at her. The impact of the shot knocked her backwards hard, her head pounding against the deck.

"Aki!" Gray shouted.

Jane swung out of the tactical chair like an acrobat, her outstretched legs kicking the gun of the second soldier out of his hand before he could even move. Then, in the same motion, she spun and smashed a fist directly into his face, sending him up and over the back of his chair.

Ryan smashed into the soldier who had fired at the same moment Gray moved. The guy fired again, the bullet hitting Ryan's helmet on the floor beside Aki.

"Hold on!" Neil shouted from the cockpit.

At that moment Neil twisted the transport up almost on its side, trying to squeeze through an opening between two giant Meta Phantoms.

Gray grabbed a chair as both of General Hein's men were smashed against the left wall.

Jane was braced against her station, and Ryan stayed beside Gray, also still on his feet in the wildly tilted room.

The guy Jane had kicked was still out cold, but the other one rolled and came up with his back against the wall and his gun pointed at Gray and Jane and Ryan.

"That's enough," he said, his back pressed against the wall holding him up as Neil kept the transport in a tight bank. "Hands where I can see them! Now!"

"Shit!" Neil shouted from the cockpit. "Everyone to my right!"

Gray wanted to turn to see the problem, but at the same time he didn't want to take his eyes off the gun the soldier in front of him was holding. Everyone but the guy with the gun was to the right side of the transport.

Suddenly part of a Meta Phantom came through the wall, swept down the side of the ship, and disappeared out the back. It happened so fast, like a weird green and red light flashing on and then off.

It barely missed Gray, Jane, and Ryan, but passed right through the soldier holding the gun.

The blue of the man's spirit seemed to jump from the armor, then be sucked out through the wall of the ship.

"Yeah!" Neil shouted from the cockpit. "We're clear! Everyone all right back there?"

No one answered as the man holding the gun stood, braced against the wall for a moment. Gray knew he was dead. The guy's spirit was gone, taken by the Meta.

Slowly, as Neil brought the transport back around level, the soldier crumpled to the ground, his helmet banging hard against the floor, the pistol still frozen in his grip.

"Couldn't have happened to a nicer guy," Ryan said, moving to check to make sure he was dead.

Gray spun and knelt beside Aki. She was still breathing, but her heartbeat felt weak. The chestplate still showed the alien particles, still seemingly agitated. On the upper corner, right over her heart, a bullet was imbedded in the metal of the plate, as if it had hit a bullet-proof vest. As far as Gray could tell, she wasn't bleeding underneath at all.

"Neil, get us back to New York," Gray said. "Fast!"

"She all right?" Jane asked, dropping back into her tactical chair.

"I have no idea," Gray said. And he didn't.

He looked down at the holographic image on Aki's chestplate. The alien particles inside her were twisting and fighting to kill the woman he loved. And there wasn't a damned thing he could do about it.

chapter 12

The view of the city under the barrier was spectacular from General Hein's office. It was one of the perks he enjoyed, and never got tired of it. He even had his desk turned to face the massive window, so that the orange glow from the barrier would always shine on him. It was a constant reminder that humans lived inside and with constant fear. And if he had his way, he was going to see the day when that barrier no longer existed. Then his office would truly have a great view of the open countryside.

And if he could just fire the Zeus weapon, he knew for a fact that day would be soon.

He watched as, on the top of a building just below his window, three men worked on the escape pods based there. The pods were ten-person ships that covered most of the tops of the tall buildings in the city. Each pod needed a basically trained pilot and could hold ten adults. They were designed to reach low orbit and stay there until ships came to rescue the inhabitants. The pods were the only way anyone could come up with to evacuate the city in case the barrier fell or was breached. Everyone had an assigned escape pod they were supposed to report to, and drills were held, sector by sector, around the city every week.

If he could just fire the Zeus cannon and get rid of the main nest of Phantoms, the escape drills would be another fact of life people would no longer have to live with.

A knock on the door broke into his thoughts.

"Come in," he said, glancing back at the paperwork in front of him. It was nothing important.

Major Elliot stepped through the door and saluted.

General Hein returned the salute and stared at the man. "Well?"

"The Deep Eyes are returning from the wasteland, sir," Major Elliot said. "Apparently there was an incident."

General Hein forced himself to keep a smile from making it to his face. This was what he had planned and hoped would happen. "What kind of incident?"

"It would seem," Major Elliot said, "that the Phantoms were attracted to Dr. Ross."

"Attracted to her?" General Hein asked. This was even better than he had hoped it would be. The Council would never allow her to roam free now. And Dr. Sid's work would be condemned to failure.

The Major nodded. "Yes, sir. The crew barely escaped with their lives. But it seems that Captain Edwards is still in command."

"How?" General Hein asked. He'd sent three of his best men with that mission. He knew the Deep Eyes were good, but his men should have had the drop on them.

"I don't know," Major Elliot said.

"I want an order issued," he said. "I want Captain Edwards and Dr. Ross placed under arrest."

"Understood," Major Elliot said.

"And all research materials pertaining to Dr. Sid's wave theory are to be confiscated immediately. Arrest him as well."

Major Elliot stared at him for a moment, clearly not understanding what he had just said.

"Do you have a problem with my orders, Major?"

"Sir," Major Elliot said, "the Council might not be too happy with that action."

General Hein got to his feet and moved over to stare out the window, his back to the major. "Ah, what a tragedy that would be. This kind of thing is exactly what I've been waiting for. The good captain and Dr. Ross have opened the door for us."

He turned to stare at Major Elliot.

"I still don't understand, sir," Elliot said.

Hein shook his head at the stupidity of some of the people around him. "Major, by tomorrow morning, the Council will be at our feet, thanking us for exposing the traitors in our midst. Dr. Sid's work attracts Phantoms instead of destroying them. The Council will implore us to use the Zeus Cannon and save them from the Phantoms. Now, follow my orders. Dismissed."

The major snapped off a salute, turned, and left.

General Hein looked back out over the city and the

barrier covering it. In a beautiful house on the hill to his left, his wife and daughter should be getting ready for dinner. But, instead, they were lying dead outside San Francisco, their life drained from them by Phantoms.

He pushed the images away, turned, and headed for the door. Maybe he would help Major Elliot with the task at hand. The sooner every Phantom was wiped from the planet, the better.

And that day would be a wonderful day. On that day he would return to San Francisco and give his family the proper burial they deserved.

Aki was unmoving in his arms as Gray hauled her into the treatment center at a dead run. Neil had made record time getting the transport back to New York, and Gray had called ahead to Dr. Sid so he would be ready and waiting.

Around him Deep Eyes ran guard, making sure that none of General Hein's men stopped them. They were lucky so far. Clearly the general hadn't expected them back this soon.

Dr. Sid and his assistant were waiting when Gray burst through the treatment room with Aki in his arms. Dr. Sid pointed to an operating table, already prepped and waiting.

As Gray laid her gently down on her back, Dr. Sid moved over her. "Did you get the seventh spirit?"

"Right here, doc," Ryan said, holding up the old ovopack.

"Good," Dr. Sid said.

Gray motioned for Jane and Neil to take up posts

outside the door. They knew enough, without him having to tell them, to not let anyone in there, no matter who it was.

Gray stayed over Aki, watching the doctor work. Clearly Aki was in bad shape. Her breathing was shallow and her face and skin were the white of the dead.

"How is she?" he finally asked, not being able to stand the silence in the room.

The doctor looked up at him. Gray could tell at once that the news was not good.

"She is dying," he said.

"But there must be something you can do," Gray said.

The doctor pointed at her chest shield and the holo-images of the phantom particles inside her. "Aki is fighting with only six of the eight spirits. We'll have to implant the seventh directly into her chestplate."

"It took a bullet," Gray said, pointing to the spot above her heart. "I think it might be damaged."

The doctor studied the bullet impact area, then looked at Gray. "I have to repair that at once."

"What can I do to help?" Gray asked.

The doctor looked up at him again, then nodded. "Actually, there is something you can do."

"Name it," Gray said.

"You may not be so fast to act when you hear what it is," the doctor said.

Gray couldn't imagine anything he wouldn't do for Aki, including giving his life. "Just tell me what to do."

The doctor nodded. "Aki's vital signs are dropping. She is slipping away from us."

"Not the words I want to hear," Gray said.

"I know that," the doctor said. "What she needs right now is a sympathetic spirit to help hold her in this world." He smiled at Gray and then went on. "I can think of no spirit better suited for that task than yours, Captain."

"I don't understand," Gray said. And he didn't. How could his spirit hold her in this world? He had no idea what the doctor was talking about.

Dr. Sid moved him around the operating table and had him lay down next to her. "You don't need to understand, Captain. You just go be with her now. And you keep her with us. That is your job."

Gray looked into the doctor's eyes and nodded. "I'll do it."

"Good," the doctor said.

Gray turned to Ryan. "Make sure the doctor is not disturbed, no matter what it takes. Understand?"

"Understood," Ryan said. "Good luck, Captain." He stepped through the door to tell Jane and Neil.

"Ready," Gray said to the doctor's assistant. He reached out and took Aki's limp hand as the assistant put a mask over his face.

"Keep her with us," the doctor said.

"You can count on it," Gray said.

He had no idea what the doctor meant, or how he was going to do what he had just promised, but he would do whatever they wanted him to do for Aki.

A moment later he closed his eyes and the operating room sounds vanished as he fell asleep, the feeling of Aki's skin against his the last thing he thought about.

chapter 13

Gray had never seen anything like it before. An alien-looking sun filled the sky, and a massive moon seemed to hang impossibly low on the horizon. It was hotter than it had been in the wasteland, even though he wasn't wearing armor. Instead, he found he had on his normal T-shirt and jeans and tennis shoes. How he had changed clothes, he didn't know.

Around him the surface looked a lot like the waste-land they had just come from, only alien. Instead of human remains and the wrecks of human vehicles, there were alien ships and the blasted trunks of strange trees.

Where the hell was he?

Where had Dr. Sid sent him? He turned completely around, looking at everything.

And how? None of this made sense.

"Gray?" Aki asked.

He jerked and spun around. She was standing beside

him. She hadn't been there a moment before, he was sure.

"Where are we?" Gray asked, glad he had found her. Or at least thought he had found her.

"On an alien planet," Aki said. She glanced at the wreck of an alien ship of some sort. "Weird place, isn't it?"

There was no doubt she was right. The weird sun, the massive moon, the alien landscape. There was no place on Earth like this, that was for sure. "How is this possible?"

She shrugged. "I'm not entirely sure."

"You seem pretty calm about this," Gray said, trying to slow his own breathing and fast-beating heart. He was feeling far from calm. The last place he had expected to end up when he got on that table with Aki was on an alien planet.

She laughed. "I guess I am. I've been having this dream every night for months."

"Dream?" Gray asked. He had no idea how he could be inside her dream. And this didn't feel like a dream. This felt very, very real.

"Well, whatever it is," Aki said. She looked at him, into his eyes. "You're really here, aren't you?"

He nodded. "I think so."

"What's happening to me?" she asked. "Back in the real world."

"We escaped the Phantoms and got you to New York. Dr. Sid is implanting the seventh spirit directly into your body right now."

Aki's face lit up at his words. He hadn't seen her look that happy in a long time. "Then you're here for me. You're my spiritual support? Gray, how sweet of you."

She moved to hug him and he let her. She felt real. Her touch seemed real. Yet around them was an alien place.

"This is a serious situation, you know," he said, looking into her eyes.

She nodded as she pulled away, still smiling. "I know it must be, but it just makes me happy that you're here with me. Someone else needs to see this."

"I'm not leaving," Gray said.

"Oh, in a minute you might wish you could," Aki said.

Gray looked at her as, under him, the ground began to shake and from over the nearby hill a rumbling filled the air.

General Hein watched as a half-dozen of his most trusted men, under the leadership of Major Elliot, ransacked Dr. Ross's laboratory on her ship. So far they had found nothing, and that was making the general more and more angry with each passing moment. No scientist could get by all these years without records of her work. The question was, where had Dr. Sid and Dr. Ross hidden their notes?

He had decided to first look on the ship they had impounded. Hein knew the Deep Eyes transport had landed a few minutes before. More than likely they were all in a treatment room near the transport. After he got done with this lab, they would go and take care of Captain Gray and Dr. Ross.

One of the soldiers accidentally activated a hidden holo-image on Dr. Ross's desk. Major Elliot took one look at it and then called out, "General, I think there's something here you should see."

General Hein moved over and looked at the holographic image being projected into the air. It was of a barren place, with an alien sun, a large moon, and alien landscape.

"And I am watching exactly *what,* Major?"

Major Elliot tapped a button on the hidden projector and the words "Dream File" appeared over the scene. It showed that she had recorded it while in orbit, just before she had dropped into old New York City.

Major Elliot turned to General Hein, a smile on his face. "It seems, sir, that Dr. Ross has been recording her dreams."

Hein looked at the alien images, the strange machines wrecked on the landscape, wondering why the major was smiling. "And why would I be interested in her dreams?"

The moment he asked the question, he knew the answer. "That's it!" he said, patting the major on the back. "This is our evidence that she is under the influence of the Phantoms."

"That it is," Major Elliot said.

"Nice work," General Hein said.

"Dr. Ross's dreams, combined with the attraction the Phantoms had to her on the excursion into the wasteland, should be more than enough for the Council to authorize the firing of the Zeus Cannon."

"I don't think so," Hein said, a plan forming quickly in his mind. "The Council is content to hide cowering inside this barrier, while the world dies a little more every day."

"So what do you plan to do?" the major asked, the smile dropping from his face.

General Hein laughed. "Oh, I just believe they need a push in the right direction."

Major Elliot nodded and said nothing.

"Get together a group of your most trusted men," General Hein said. "Then report to me. Bring this evidence and then destroy this lab before you leave, equipment and everything."

"Understood," Major Elliot said.

General Hein turned and headed for the door. This was working out better than he could have hoped.

The rumbling grew louder from the other side of the hill as Gray stood and stared. It was as if the entire alien world was about to rip apart. Then, as he watched, a massive alien army stormed over the hills, bearing down on them from all sides, for as far as he could see. It was the most frightening thing he had seen in a long time. Most of the aliens wore shining armor that glinted in the bright sun. To his trained eye, they were working together, as a fighting unit thousands strong.

He studied them. Each carried a strange-looking weapon.

"We've got to get out of here!" he shouted to Aki over the noise.

She shook her head and pointed in the other direction.

He turned to look where she was pointing. There he could hear another rumbling, building and matching the first. And a moment later a second alien army swarmed over that horizon, also heading for them.

This army wore different armor, different colors, and

were shaped slightly differently. And they looked just as angry.

He and Aki were caught between them, yet she didn't seem concerned.

The two alien armies were screaming at each other, firing on each other with laser-like weapons and massive cannons. They were alien soldiers that reminded Gray of different Phantom shapes. But these were clearly not Phantoms.

The two armies smashed into each other, fighting hand-to-hand, sometimes so close that Gray thought he could reach out and touch a soldier. He had seen video of the old world wars, before the Phantoms. But even those images weren't as horrific as this battle.

And none of it seemed to actually touch them at all. It was as if a bubble was over them, protecting them.

Beside him Aki watched the fight going on around them, not even looking upset. It was as if she was just waiting for it to be over. How could she have become so complacent to such carnage? Gray had no idea.

Then, suddenly, the two armies stopped fighting and turned to stare at them. Chills ran down his back as thousands of alien soldiers looked at him.

"What are they doing?" Gray asked, staring back into the alien eyes behind the armor. "Why are they staring at us?"

"Not at us," Aki said.

She turned Gray around gently and pointed at the horizon. There a wall of fire swept toward them. It was like no other fire he had seen. It stretched from the ground to the sky and as far in both directions as he could see. It was red and yellow and blue, and seemed to *have no source or power behind it. It moved like a curtain.*

As it hit the armies, they were vaporized.

Aki took his hand and grasped it firmly as the wall of flame hit them and went right over, leaving them untouched.

Aki looked down at herself, then at Gray. "The last time I got this far in this dream, I woke up convinced I had been burnt. I didn't feel anything this time. Maybe the seventh spirit made the difference."

Gray hadn't felt anything either. But clearly that hadn't been the case for the alien soldiers. Both armies had been vaporized almost instantly. Nothing now remained on the surface of the planet but the two of them and the thick dust of the dead.

Suddenly Aki and Gray are floating up off the surface of the planet.

"Has this happened before?" Gray asked, holding tightly onto her hand to keep them from floating apart.

"No," Aki said.

Below them the planet was breaking up. Massive upheavals in the crust threw magma into the air like fountains. Gray could still feel weight under him, yet they were floating, higher and higher as the planet ripped itself apart below them.

Then, for a moment, it seemed as if everything might calm down. The eruptions subsided, the lava cooled.

And then the planet's surface seemed to shrink inward, then explode, spinning off vast hunks of itself as it tore apart.

On the largest hunk of the planet a flow of billions of Phantom spirits moved up from the center of the planet and onto the hunk, burrowing inside it as the meteor sped into the blackness of space.

"Now I understand," Aki said, her voice low and filled with awe.

Gray was just about to ask what it was she understood when he was pulled away from her, his hand yanked from hers, as a bright light swept over him and took him from her before he could even think of resisting.

chapter 14

Gray forced open his eyes, the bright light hurting them. But he had to see where he was, why he had been taken from Aki.

Dr. Sid moved in to block the light. Suddenly Gray remembered where he was, where he had started from before ending up on the strange planet, getting mowed down by aliens and a wall of fire.

He looked down. His hand was still holding Aki's beside him. It had all been some sort of dream. Or nightmare. Definitely a nightmare.

Dr. Sid's smile was a relief to his frazzled nerves. "Welcome back, Captain."

Gray moved carefully, easing his legs over the edge and sitting. Aki still lay beside him, her breathing easy and relaxed.

"Is it over?" Gray asked.

Dr. Sid nodded. "It is."

"How is she?"

"She's going to be fine," he said, smiling. "But this is only temporary."

"She needs the eighth spirit," Gray said.

"Exactly," the doctor said, helping Gray down off the table. "We need it to cure her completely."

Gray glanced at where Neil stood just inside the door. "Any problems?"

"Nothing yet, Captain," Neil said, smiling. "Glad you made it back."

"Glad to be back," Gray said as the images of the alien planet flashed through his mind. He sure didn't want to go back there any time soon. How had Aki stood those dreams?

"Stand down and tell the others to come in."

"Will do, Captain," Neil said, looking relieved.

Gray turned to face Aki. She looked tired, but fine. The shield over her chest was covered with a blouse, with only a sliver of metal showing below the neck. He glanced over at Dr. Sid. "All right to try to wake her?"

"Go ahead," the doctor said.

Gray leaned down and gently touched her cheek. Her skin was warn and soft. "Aki? Can you hear me?"

Slowly, she began to stir. Behind him Gray heard the Deep Eyes come in and gather around the table, watching.

Aki slowly opened her eyes and Dr. Sid shut off the bright operating table light as she did. She blinked a few times, then looked at Dr. Sid and Gray and smiled.

"I finished it," she said.

"Finished what?" Dr. Sid asked.

"The dream," she said, her smile getting bigger. "I know what it means. I know what the Phantoms really are."

Gray remembered the dream as well, at least the part he had seen, and he had no idea what she was talking about. The armies had fought and died; the planet had exploded. What was she talking about?

Behind him the operating-room doors burst open and Hein's men charged in, wearing full battle gear.

Gray turned to see a half dozen weapons covering them.

"Stand down," Gray ordered his men as Neil started to bring up his rifle.

"Nobody move!" one of the soldiers shouted.

"Nobody's moving," Gray said. The last thing he wanted was to lose one of his men stupidly, let alone Aki and Dr. Sid.

"You are all under arrest!" the soldier said as the Deep Eyes all dropped their weapons.

"Well, that's a surprise," Dr. Sid said, shaking his head. "I'll wager this is General Hein's doing. Just once I'd love to have a military mind have an original thought."

"Not sure how to take that, Doc," Gray said.

Dr. Sid laughed. "Present company excluded, of course."

General Hein sat at his desk. The blinds over the window had been drawn and the room's anti-bugging equipment was turned on. In front of his desk were Major Elliot and seven other soldiers. They were men he could trust completely. And soon would.

Major Elliot snapped off a small communicator and looked at the general. "We have them, sir."

The general knew that Elliot was expecting a positive response, but he didn't bother. There was no doubt that Captain Edwards and the Deep Eyes would be captured. They wouldn't fight other soldiers. It wasn't in their nature. And in this city, there really wasn't any place to run or hide.

"Sir?" Major Elliot said.

Hein looked at the major and the other soldiers and knew it was time to start. "My wife and daughter were killed by Phantoms when the San Francisco barrier city was attacked. Did I ever tell you that?"

Major Elliot looked stunned. He shook his head no.

The other soldiers seemed uneasy learning such personal information about him. But that was what he wanted. He needed them to feel as if he was just like them.

"I try to imagine," General Hein said, going on with his little speech, "what that must have been like, seeing everyone around you fall over dead for no apparent reason."

Now the major was really squirming.

"And then, at the end, feeling something next to you, invisible, touching you, reaching inside your body, pulling the life from you and your child."

He stood and leaned over the desk right into Major Elliot's face. "You've lost family, haven't you?"

"Yes, sir," Major Elliot said.

The general looked at the other men. All of them were nodding.

He knew they would be. He knew more about each

of them then they thought he knew. He wasn't going to trust this plan to anyone who wasn't thinking completely with him.

"Good," he said. "That's why I trust all of you. You all know what must be done."

They all nodded, even though none of them had a clue what he was intending. But they soon would.

He moved around the desk and headed for the door with the men following. Time to put the last part of his plan into action. By the morning, the Council would listen to every word he said. And that would be the start of ending this war.

It took them just under twenty minutes to descend into the Barrier Generator facility. It was a massive complex of heavy machinery and glowing green ovo-energy pipes that lead to the very core of the place.

It was the Barrier Generator, as this complex was called, that kept the city protected from the Phantoms. And right now it was the exact place he needed to be to start what he knew would be the end for the Phantoms.

At the main security door Major Elliot ran his security card through the scanner and punched in the correct code. Inside a nearby booth, the general knew two men were scanning them, seeing who he was.

A moment later the heavy security doors opened.

As his troop got through, he ordered, "Major, arrest these men."

It took a moment and some complaints from the dozen workers in the facility, but finally they were all rounded up and escorted out the door. Then the door was closed and secured. "No one through," he said to two of his men. "Period."

He turned his attention back to the main control room. A massive map of the entire city and all the barrier sectors covered one wall. At the moment everything was green, showing normal ovo-energy flow and activity. Good.

He had his remaining five soldiers take stations around the room. He pointed to the main control and command chair for Major Elliot. He knew that Major Elliot had done a stint of six months in this facility and knew how to operate it all. So did the other five men he had assigned stations.

"Okay," he said to Major Elliot, "here's what I need you to do. Reduce power to Sector 31."

Major Elliot snapped around in the chair and looked at him. "Sir, do you realize that the Phantoms will—"

"What I realize, Major, is that we must force the Council to take action against the enemy. And a little scare in a sparely populated sector will do the job just fine."

The major nodded and turned back to his panel, issuing orders as he went.

"Reduce flow of alpha pipe?"

"Twenty-five percent of alpha pipe energy flow redirected," one soldier said.

"Lower output to Sector 31," Major Elliot ordered.

"Lowering output," a second soldier repeated.

On the big board a small sector turned bright red. An alarm sounded, filling the room with the whoops of the danger warning.

"Turn that damn thing off," he ordered.

Major Elliot did as he was ordered, and silence again filled the room.

Another big board filling a second wall came to life. A moment before it had been clear. It was a map of the city as well, only this board showed Phantom activity. And there was activity starting in Sector 31.

Good. A few people would die tonight, but their sacrifice would be worth getting the Council to move and save all of humanity.

"They're coming through now, General," the major said.

"Oh, I think we can easily handle a few Phantoms in a contained space," he said. He had picked Sector 31 for the simple reason that the entire area was easily shut off from the rest of the city. And right now that was being done by the military.

The major glanced up at the big board showing the incursion of Phantoms, then back at the general.

"Relax, Major, when the night's over, you're going to be a hero."

General Hein watched as, on the big board, the opening in the Sector 31 barrier blinked a flashing red.

And on the other wall, the Phantoms were spreading into the sector.

His plan was working perfectly.

Now it was only a matter of time.

chapter 15

The cell block was more comfortable than Aki had imagined it might be. It had high ceilings, white corridors with bright lights chasing any chance of a shadow away, and no other inmates besides them in the cell block. The cells were open onto the corridor, with simple lines in the air. She had been told by Gray that those lines marked pulsonic lasers. There was no getting through them.

Each cell was large, about twenty feet across, with beds, a small desk, a toilet, and a sink, all built into the thick walls. Security cameras dotted the ceiling of the hallway, clearly able to see every inch of every cell.

Aki had no doubt they were being very carefully watched by General Hein's men at that very moment.

Gray, Aki, and Dr. Sid had all been put together in one cell along the right side of the hallway, while the three members of Deep Eyes had the cell facing them on the left. Since there was no one else in the cell block at all, they could talk freely.

Since they had arrived and gotten settled, Aki had been telling them about her dream, and about what she thought it meant. At the moment she was sitting cross-legged on the floor in front of her cell door. She could see Neil across the way, lying on his bunk. Jane leaned against one wall of her cell, and Ryan sat on the floor. They seemed relaxed and not at all upset about being tossed in jail.

Gray was leaning against the wall near her, and Dr. Sid was sitting on the bed.

"Aki," Gray said, "I'm not so sure you're calling it right."

"You were in my dream, Gray," she said, looking into his eyes. "You saw the same things I did."

"That's just it," he said, his voice echoing a little down the empty cell block toward the main door. "I'm not sure what I saw. How can you be?"

"Captain, please," Dr. Sid said, holding up his hand. "Let her continue."

Aki smiled as Gray nodded. Then she went on. "All right, let's come at this a different way," she said. "Why do you think we've never been able to determine a relationship between the human-sized phantoms and the giant Metas roaming the wasteland?"

"Excuse me, Doc," Neil said from across the corridor, "but what friggin' relationship?"

"He's right," Ryan said. "You have your human-sized Phantoms, your caterpillary Phantoms, and your flying snake-like Phantoms, not to forget my personal favorite, the big giant Metas."

"Down, boy," Jane said, laughing. "We know how you really love your job, but don't go getting excited in here."

Aki laughed, as did the others. For six people jailed without cause, they were certainly an upbeat bunch.

"He's right, though," Neil said. "If you've spent as much time in the field as we have, you know there is no relationship between any of them. It's like a zoo out there."

"Precisely," Aki said, glad that Neil had made her point. "I think those giant ones are like our whales or elephants."

"All right, so tell me," Neil said, "why would an invading army bring a bunch of whales and elephants along for the ride?"

"Some kind of crazy Noah's Ark?" Jane asked.

"You know," Dr. Sid said, breaking into the conversation from his cell, "we have always assumed the meteor was intended as a form of transportation. Perhaps it wasn't."

"The meteor is a chunk of their planet," Aki said, remembering how at the end of her dream the planet was breaking apart, and one large chunk was shooting off into space.

"But how could they survive the trip across outer space on a hunk of rock?" Neil asked.

"They didn't," Aki said.

There was silence in the cell block as everyone thought about her words.

"You know," Neil said, "you are starting to make a creepy kind of sense."

"I agree," Gray said, his voice soft and firm. "I think

what you are saying explains why we never had a chance when fighting them. All our strategies are based on one assumption: that we were fighting alien invaders."

"Think of the dream, Gray," Aki said. "Think of how all the aliens in the dream died. Since then all they have known is suffering. They're not an invading army. They're ghosts."

No one had anything at all to say to that.

General Hein leaned in over Major Elliot to check out the board in front of him. It showed the activity of the Phantoms entering Sector 31 on a holographic map. So far, so good. It was just about time to button things up again and then clean up the mess.

Above him, on the massive wall holograph of the entire Barrier system, Sector 31 still showed a flashing red. On the other wall holograph, the entire area of Sector 31 showed solid Phantom infestation.

"How many have entered?" Hein asked.

Major Elliot worked the board in front of him, but no exact number appeared. "Not sure, exactly sir," Elliot said. "A lot of them, from what I can tell."

"Excellent," Hein said. That was exactly what he had wanted. This would give the Council a good scare and get them moving. "Start the procedure to bring back up Sector 31's barrier. Are there squads moving in to clean up the Phantoms?"

"Yes, sir," Elliot said.

"Are they being contained?"

"So far they are, sir," Elliot said.

"Perfect," General Hein said. "Now we just wait until

it's all cleaned up. And by tomorrow, the Zeus cannon will have wiped the home nest of these creatures from the face of the planet."

Hein paced back and forth as his men worked to re-establish the barrier over Sector 31. He knew this plan would work. He had had no doubt at all. And he had been right. It was working like clockwork.

Major Elliot and the others almost had the Sector 31 barrier power back up when things went wrong.

"Sir!" Major Elliot said, panic clear in his voice, "I have numerous Phantom contacts."

"Of course you do," he said.

"Outside of Sector 31, sir," Major Elliot said, without turning away from his control panel. "And they're moving at incredible speed."

General Hein glanced up at the big board. It showed Phantom contacts moving out from Sector 31 far faster than possible. He moved over to Major Elliot.

"What the hell is going on here? I thought you said they were contained?"

"It's not a computer error, sir," he said. "I checked that first. Somehow they are moving in the pipes."

General Hein shook his head. Major Elliot wasn't making any sense at all. "What pipes?"

"Sir," Elliot said, "they're moving with the bio-etheric energy flow."

That wasn't possible. The energy flow was what powered the barriers. Phantoms couldn't move or even exist in that flow. He glanced up at the holographic map on the wall. What he saw made his entire body shake. It showed hundreds of Phantoms dispersing at an incredible speed throughout the city.

"That's impossible!" he shouted. "Nothing living could survive in those pipes."

"We've got a big one heading this way, sir," one of the men said.

Again he leaned in over the major's shoulder to study the board. The man was right. There was a large snake-like Phantom headed inbound.

And fast.

General Hein glanced around. None of his men were armed with any kind of weapon that could fight a Phantom. They only wore their bullet-firing side arms. And never had a bullet stopped a Phantom.

Also, none of these men had any real experience with Phantoms. They had dealt with humans, leaving the Phantom fighting to the likes of Captain Gray and his men.

Through the window the energy in the pipes illuminated the long, massive Phantom as it got closer.

"Oh, my god," Major Elliot said, staring at it.

Two of the other men started to raise their pistols to fire at the snake inside the energy pipe.

"Hold your fire!" he shouted at them as the snake disappeared through the flooring. "Are you nuts?"

They both looked terrified, but somehow they managed to retake their positions again.

Was he the only one around there who could think? The bullets from their pistols wouldn't hurt the Phantom, but they might break open the energy pipes, killing them all even faster than the Phantom would.

"Get Sector 31 buttoned up!" he ordered. "Do it fast! We can still keep this under control if we move quickly."

The men jumped back to work, racing to complete the process they had already started. Suddenly the snake came up out of the floor, its shape vaguely illuminated by the light from the ovo-pipes. It snapped around the man sitting at the energy controls, flowing through him as if he wasn't there.

The man stiffened and then slumped forward, dead. The Phantom had taken the life out of him instantly.

A soldier to Hein's right opened fire on the snake with his pistol, and two others did the same.

"Hold your fire!" Hein shouted, ducking as the bullets bounced around the room. The snake turned and headed for the three men and they kept firing, backing up as they went.

The rounds from their guns pounded into the control panels, sending smoke and parts flying, but doing nothing to the snake-like Phantom.

"Cease fire, damn it!" General Hein shouted.

They finally complied as the Phantom dropped down through the floor again, but the damage had been done. One of the main boards had been hit, and the ovo-tank it controlled started to react to the sudden fluctuation.

Suddenly, beyond the window of the control room, in the massive main pumping room, there was a muffled explosion as one of the pipelines burst, causing the next, and then the next to let go.

Red lights started to fill the board as, around the city, sector after sector of the barrier failed.

General Hein watched in horror as the lights flickered and went out, plunging the room into darkness.

Another of his men screamed as the Phantom tore the life force from his body.

A moment later the emergency lights came up. Emergency power flickered back into the panels and the map on the wall lit up again, showing that most of the barrier over the entire city was gone.

Oh, God, what had he done?

Two of the soldiers began to fire at the snake again as Major Elliot worked at the emergency-powered board, trying to do anything to get the barrier up again.

Suddenly one of the bullets bounced off a panel and hit the major squarely in the chest. Hein watched as the major slumped out of the chair, a hand covered in blood pressed to his chest.

"What happened?" the major asked.

"It went wrong," Hein said. Then, as he watched, the light went out of the major's eyes.

The Phantom came up out of the flooring and swiped the solider standing beside General Hein, killing him instantly. The man slumped to the floor on top of the major.

General Hein turned. It was time to get out of here and out of the city. He ran for the door. "Open it and get out!" he shouted to the man inside the booth.

The last man inside the door-security control room punched the door open just as the Phantom came up and killed him.

Beyond the main window of the control room another ovo-tank exploded in flashes of bright orange and blue light. General Hein knew there was no saving this city now. He had destroyed it.

And killed everyone in it.

Hein ran from the control room and onto the emergency elevator as the computer-activated voice repeated over and over the nearest evacuation point.

If he was lucky, he'd make it to the military evac area. But at that moment he wasn't sure he wanted to.

chapter 16

The conversation in the cell block had almost ceased. Gray was even starting to believe Aki's point of view about the dream and the Phantoms. It sure explained a great deal. No wonder humans had had such a problem fighting the Phantoms. Humans had always thought of them as an invading army, when really they were nothing more than a bunch of ghosts. Very deadly and unhappy ghosts, but ghosts nonetheless.

And with that information now in their hands, Dr. Sid and Aki needed to get out of there and talk to the Council. Everything needed to change.

"Come on, Neil," Gray said to his man directly across from him. "We need to think of a way out. Now you're our man, so don't let me down. Think."

He smiled at the shocked look on Neil's face. "Captain, these walls are titanium alloy and the bars are pulsonic lasers."

"So?" Gray asked, smiling at Neil.

"So?" Neil asked. "It's not as if I can just wave a magic wand and—"

As Neil waved his arm in the air, the lights flickered and the cell doors slid opened.

"Hold your positions, everyone!" Gray ordered. He had no idea what had just happened, but he didn't like the looks of it.

He stood and cautiously stepped out into the hall. It wouldn't be beyond General Hein to shoot them in a made-up jail break, just to get rid of them. At this point anything was possible.

He glanced down the hallway toward the main door, which had also swung open. From the looks of this, some sort of automatic release system had been triggered. And the only thing that would do that would be Phantoms loose inside the barrier.

That thought made him shudder.

He waited. His men stood ready to move.

No one said a word.

No guard appeared. This sure didn't have the makings of a trap. And if it wasn't a trap, then Phantoms *were* in the city.

"Clear," Gray said. "I think we had better get moving."

Aki stepped out and looked at him with a puzzled frown.

"Neil," Gray said, "I'm impressed at your magical abilities with hand-waving."

Neil grunted as he stepped into the hall. "That makes two of us."

Suddenly a computer voice filled the hallway. "Please

proceed to the nearest evacuation facility. Proceed to the nearest evacuation facility."

Over and over the message repeated as they all stood there, shocked.

It was worse than Gray had even feared. Parts of the barrier had to be completely down if they were ordering an evacuation of the entire city.

Aki and Dr. Sid looked stunned, their faces white.

Neil nodded, repeating the computer message that droned on and on. "I think we should proceed to the nearest evacuation facility."

"Great idea," Gray said.

"What do you think has happened?" Dr. Sid asked.

"I don't know," Gray said, "but it can't be good."

"I thought Dr. Sid was the master of understatements," Neil said.

When they reached the center area of the cell block, there was no one to be seen, and no weapons that would be of any use against a Phantom. The light over the emergency elevator was blinking green and the door was standing open, waiting. Emergency elevators were only used in times like this. They were high speed and only had one stop, the top level where the evacuation pods were supposed to be.

Gray herded them all into the elevator and punched the button. The force of the fast lift pushed against them. Dr. Sid would have dropped to his knees if Aki hadn't held him up.

The quick stop at the top almost left them weightless. The door slid open and they all piled out onto a long catwalk as behind them the elevator closed and dropped back to its ready position in the cell block.

A computer voice told them how to get to the nearest escape-pod launching sight as they moved away from the building and stopped.

The catwalk overlooked the entire city. Gray was stunned at what he saw. The entire barrier was gone, the energy-towers sticking into the sky like candles in a cake. There were large explosions coming from the center that powered the barrier, sending blue light over everything. That ovo-energy light was making the Phantoms visible to the naked eye, and they seemed to be everywhere, both on the ground and in the air.

People were running through the streets below, and escape pods rose from throughout the city, their jets taking survivors to safety. Gray knew there weren't enough pods for everyone, but with this type of massive barrier failure, most of the population would be dead before they reached a pod.

The nearest pods from this point were across the catwalk and up three floors. From what he could see, two of the five pods there were already launched and there were more people up there than the remaining pods could handle. That wasn't going to be a route they could take to escape.

"Man," Neil said, "we need some weapons."

"And we need to get to my ship," Aki said, staring at the mob scene on the rooftop across from them.

Dr. Sid nodded. "I agree. That's the safest place we could be right now."

"I bet it was towed into the city," Neil said. "It would be in the military hanger."

"I'm sure it is," Gray said. "I saw the report on it."

"So we go there," Aki said.

Below them a massive explosion shook the catwalk. Bright yellow and orange flames shot out everywhere, covering entire buildings. Gray had no doubt that, just as with the original New York, this New York was doomed. Maybe some day there would be a third.

"You're right," Gray said. "Let's go."

They had almost made the first bank of regular elevators of the building they had been jailed in when Neil shouted, "Here they come!"

The Phantoms seemed to emerge from everywhere around them. Most of them were the size of humans, with flowing odd forms visible because of the ovo-energy covering the area.

Suddenly one of them came up through the floor of the catwalk, almost in the middle of the group. Since Gray and Aki had been leading, they were cut off from the rest of the group as everyone moved to get out of the way.

The Phantom hesitated, then turned toward Gray and Aki.

"Meet at the hanger!" Gray shouted.

Ryan nodded, twisted Dr. Sid around, and started running back the way they had come.

Gray grabbed Aki's arm and pulled her as fast as they could run down the hall and then out along a covered walkway to another building as the Phantom moved to follow them.

"But the others?" Aki shouted over an explosion below. "And Dr. Sid!"

"The Deep Eyes will take care of him!" Gray shouted back. At the moment he was much more concerned about the two of them. Without a weapon of any sort, the only hope they had was avoiding the Phantoms they could see. He just hoped there weren't any they couldn't see. They would never know it if there were.

At the bank of elevators at an intersection of three corridors in the next building, they both pushed the down buttons frantically. The normal elevators never seemed to arrive when he needed one, and right now was no exception.

"Gray!" Aki said, grabbing his arm and pointing at a Phantom coming down the hall slowly at them. This building had been some sort of office complex, and the Phantom was far bigger than the wide hall.

Gray punched the down button again, then looked for a place they could run. There was another Phantom halfway down the hall to the left, so that wasn't going to work. The right corridor looked clear, but for how long?

Finally, one of the elevator doors slid open with a ding that was barely audible over the explosions.

Gray yanked Aki inside and hit the button for the train-station level, and then the door-closed button, watching as the Phantom kept coming and coming.

It seemed as if the door would never close. With the Phantom less than ten meters away, finally the door slid closed. Gray pulled Aki to the very back of the elevator as the Phantom drifted through the door, coming right at them. It was just about to pass over both of them, killing them instantly, when the elevator dropped.

The Phantom disappeared through the ceiling.

"Too close," Aki said, letting out a breath she had been holding. "Why are we able to see them, even in the elevator?"

"I don't know," Gray said. "Maybe they are carrying residual charges from the ovo-energy explosions."

"That would make sense," Aki said. "At least we're safe for the moment."

"Just hope the elevator doesn't pass through one on the way down."

"I wish you hadn't said that." They both stared at the floor the entire rest of the way down.

The door opened with another ding. A computer voice said, "Trains are not operating. We apologize for the inconvenience."

Gray eased himself into the doorway of the elevator, blocking the door open. The station platform was like a battlefield of horror. Corpses were piled on top of each other, and the staircase leading to the next level was at least six or seven deep with bodies.

"Oh, no," Aki said, her voice soft.

A train car had been at the station when the barrier dropped. A dozen bodies were still in the closest car, and on one car an automatic door was opening and closing on a body, the computer voice repeating over and over: "Please stand out of the door."

"We've got to move," Gray said, pulling Aki out of the elevator. He grabbed a middle-aged man's body and pulled him a few feet to block open the elevator in case they needed it.

Then, carefully, trying to step around the bodies where the could, they headed for the far end of the train. They hadn't gone more than twenty steps when a Phantom came up out of the floor, as if it were coming right out of a body.

"Damn," Gray said.

Another Phantom, and then another appeared. They were trapped and there was just no way out of there. They were going to have to try their luck on another level.

"Back to the elevator," Gray said as three of the Phantoms started toward them.

Suddenly, from the right, there was a loud crash and an armored jeep smashed down the staircase, shoving bodies aside as it came.

Gray could not believe his eyes. Neil was behind the wheel, with Dr. Sid holding on for dear life in the passenger seat. Ryan and Jane had weapons, and the minute the jeep hit the terminal floor they opened up on the approaching Phantoms, vaporizing them instantly.

"All aboard, Captain!" Ryan shouted as Neil slid the jeep to a halt, scattering bodies in all directions.

Ryan tossed him a rifle as they climbed on board, then handed another one to Aki.

Jane was still firing as more and more Phantoms came up out of the floor, through the bodies.

Neil hit the gas, the jeep bumping over the dead as it left the platform and landed down on the rail tracks in the direction the stalled train had been heading.

"Where'd you find the equipment?" Gray shouted over the noise of Jane firing to keep their path clear and the jeep bouncing on the rough tracks.

"Council security headquarters," Ryan said. "Dr. Sid

figured they wouldn't be using it since they had already evacuated. And it was close by. Just luck."

Gray just shook his head. Sometimes it was better to be lucky than good. To make it to Aki's ship, even with weapons and a jeep, they were going to need a lot of luck.

chapter 17

General Hein stood on a catwalk near the top of one of the tallest buildings in the city. Below him the city was dying—one fire, one explosion, one life at a time. His mind wouldn't let him turn away and walk to the military shuttle behind him on the roof. He had to see what he had caused. So he stood and watched as dozens and dozens of people pushed forward on a platform on the top of the building below him, trying to force their way into one of six escape pods that would take them to safety.

There were hundreds of the pods on similar platforms around the city, all on the tops of tall buildings, always ready to be launched. But the escape pods could only carry so many people, usually ten at most, and needed a pilot to fly them. One out of every ten citizens in the city had been trained to fly the pods, but that didn't mean that one of those pilots got on every pod.

And clearly the people already on the pods were not waiting. They were launching the pods in panic, overloaded and without pilots, hoping to reach orbit and safety one way or another.

General Hein knew the pods didn't work that way. Without someone with training, the escape pods wouldn't make it above the old barrier height. As he watched, for every escape pod that lifted clear and shot into the night sky, another two went out of control and smashed into buildings or streets.

On the roof below, screams brought his attention back to the scene in front of him. A Phantom had come up out of the floor near one pod-loading area, killing three people almost instantly.

Hundreds started screaming and pushing, climbing over each other to get out of the way as the Phantom floated through person after person, leaving them nothing but a dead husk of flesh, their life forces robbed from their bodies.

The pod closest to the Phantom slammed its door and a moment later lifted.

Or tried to lift.

General Hein watched the fruitless attempt as the pod, with far too many people on board, didn't even reach his level, but instead veered hard right, exploding and crashing into the middle of a street many stories below.

Another Phantom came up out of the top of the building, killing more people. There was no place for the people to run to.

He turned away. He couldn't watch another death.

He moved to the military shuttle standing ready and walked up the ramp to get on board.

A soldier saluted, but he ignored the salute. Instead he turned toward the room reserved for him down the short hallway.

Behind him he heard the hatch of the shuttle slam shut. This bird could carry a hundred more to safety, but it held only him and the crew. That was a hundred more lives he was responsible for taking.

He closed the door to his private room as a voice came over the intercom. "Please strap into your seat, General. Five seconds to liftoff."

He automatically did as instructed, not really thinking or caring. All he could think about was how his wife and daughter had died when the San Francisco city barrier had been attacked. How many wives and daughters of other men had he killed today?

He closed his eyes, but the images of all those deaths were like ghosts drifting through his mind, taking his soul just as a Phantom would take his life.

He didn't even notice when the shuttle lifted to the safe harbor of Earth orbit.

For the moment the tracks were clear of Phantoms, and Jane wasn't firing from the top of the armored jeep. The only sound was the tires pounding over the rough tracks. Aki was forcing herself to take deep breaths, trying to calm down enough to think. So far they had managed to get out of the detention center and find weapons and transportation. But that was a long way from getting to her ship and into orbit.

"This line doesn't take us directly to the military hanger," Ryan said to Gray.

"I know," Gray said, pointing at the windows along

the tunnel that were flashing past every hundred meters or so. "We're going to have to get off pretty soon."

"I don't think I like the sounds of that," Dr. Sid said.

"I don't, either," Neil said, smiling at Dr. Sid. "And I'm driving."

Suddenly, what looked to Aki to be an escape pod smashed down through a glass overhead and onto the transit tracks a few hundred meters in front of them. The pod, for a second, looked as if it might remain intact, then it bounced, hit the transit wall, and exploded. The concussion almost lifted the front of the jeep off the ground.

"Now's as good a time as any!" Gray shouted as the orange and red fireball rolled at them through the tunnel. "Hang on, everyone!"

Aki ducked and closed her eyes, holding on as tightly as she could to the back of the seat in front of her.

Neil yanked the jeep hard right and up over the two-foot concrete barrier that separated the sunken tracks from the station platform. Then, without slowing, he smashed through a massive plate glass window and into a wide hallway-like area just as the fireball rolled past behind them.

Glass rained down over Aki as they slid sideways. Neil quickly got them going straight again and then slowed.

"Clear!" Gray said. "Nice job, Neil."

"All in a day's driving."

Aki looked up.

Gray was brushing glass out of his hair. Dr. Sid, in the front seat, looked more shocked than anything else. Jane was back in her position, standing behind Aki, rifle at ready.

Aki brushed the glass off of her pants and out of her hair, then looked around. The place they had crashed into had high ceilings and a smooth, covered road down the middle. The sidewalks on either side were lined with potted trees. Skylights were spaced overhead to let in daylight. It looked like they were in some sort of massive office complex built below street level. It had to be at least a kilometer long.

"We're inside the main military office center," Jane shouted to Gray. "I've been here before. The hangers are ahead and up to the right, beyond the main transit station."

"Got you," Neil said, keeping the armored vehicle headed down the center of the road. At the moment there were no Phantoms in sight, but there were also no other live humans. Just bodies scattered along the sidewalk.

For the moment it felt quiet, as if nothing was wrong. Then ahead of them, a few hundred meters down the long interior street, a massive Phantom floated through the roof, blocking their way entirely.

"Is that a Meta?" Ryan asked.

Gray looked stunned. "Didn't know they were this far east."

"Looks like they are now," Jane said.

Neil slid the vehicle to a stop.

"Behind us!" Jane shouted.

Aki looked around. Another huge Phantom had blocked off the direction they had just come, and was moving toward them slowly, half its body outside the roofline of the building. They were trapped, of that there was no doubt. And Aki had no idea what Gray was going to decide to do.

"Okay?" Neil asked. "Now what?"

Gray looked at the Phantom blocking their way ahead, then at the one coming up from behind. Aki watched him study the side of the building closest to them. There were no windows or doors in it. On the other side of the street was another glass window looking out over the transit tracks. That way was blocked for sure, from the crashed escape pod.

From what she could tell, the building without windows and doors was part of the main transit station. Jane had said the military hangar where the *Black Boa* was stored was on the other side of that wall.

"We're going through," Gray said.

Neil pointed at the wall in front of him. It was blank and looked pretty solid. "I don't see no doors or windows."

"What?" Dr. Sid asked. "What are we doing?"

"Captain," Ryan said from beside Jane, "with all due respect . . ."

"Excuse me, Captain," Jane said, "but we're running out of time here."

Aki glanced around. The huge Phantom was within a hundred meters of them and closing.

"The transit station," Gray said, pointing at the solid wall in front of the vehicle. "We're going through it."

Neil nodded. "It's the only way."

He jammed the vehicle into reverse and backed it almost against the window across the street from the station. To Aki's left the shape of the Phantom seemed to fill everything, it was so close.

"I gather this will be somewhat of a rough ride?" Dr. Sid asked.

"Doc," Neil said, gunning the jeep at the wall, "you *do* have a talent for understatement."

"Hang on!" Gray shouted.

Aki again ducked behind the seat, bracing herself as best she could for the crash. Out of the corner of her eye she saw Jane and Ryan in the open back of the jeep drop and do the same.

The impact felt as if someone had slammed her against concrete instead of the back of a seat. Then, for a moment, everything was weightless as the jeep got through the wall and went airborne over the floor a good five meters below. Neil somehow managed to land the jeep almost on its wheels, bouncing everyone so hard Aki thought she was going to fly out.

Then the vehicle spun like a circus ride, around and around on what turned out to be a slick, tile floor. Just when Aki thought it was all over, the jeep hit something hard and rolled once before coming to a stop on its wheels against a concrete barrier of some sort.

For a long few seconds the dust and noise settled.

Aki forced herself to take a deep breath before looking up in Gray's worried face.

"You all right?" he asked.

She wasn't sure, but she nodded anyhow. Nothing seemed broken, but after that pounding, she wouldn't be surprised if half her body had been bruised.

Neil pulled himself out from under the steering wheel. "Doc? Dr. Sid, are you all right?"

Aki pulled herself up from the floor of the back seat

with Gray's help, using the front seat as a brace. Dr. Sid was moving, and as she watched, he sat up and looked around. "Interesting."

"Another understatement, Doc," Neil said.

"Anybody hurt?" Gray asked, looking around for Ryan and Jane.

Jane was standing behind the jeep, her rifle at ready, watching the Phantom pass them beyond the wall. The room they had ended up in was massive and opened onto a huge hangar area. If they were lucky, the *Black Boa* would be very close by.

Jane walked around to the hangar side of the jeep and her face went white. "Captain!"

Gray jumped down and moved around to where she was standing. It took Aki a moment longer to follow.

There, pinned under the wreckage of what was left of the front of the jeep, was Ryan. A metal bar stuck out of his lower abdomen, and his breathing was shallow. His legs were smashed under the front of the wreck. Aki knew instantly it was going to take some quick emergency care to save him.

"Oh, God," Neil said, moving to Ryan's side. "Talk to me, Sarge."

Ryan looked up at Neil. "Ouch."

"Gimme a hand, Jane," Neil said as he and Jane and Gray moved into position around Ryan. It looked as if they were going to try to lift the jeep off him and pull him from the metal bar that was sticking through him. Aki knew instantly that wasn't going to work, but Dr. Sid spoke up before she could.

"No, wait," Dr. Sid said, moving as fast as he could to stop Gray. "You're risking further injury. We need the proper tools to cut him out of there. Otherwise you might kill him."

"I've got the tools we would need in my ship," Aki said.

Gray nodded and stood.

Dr. Sid turned and went back to the jeep. There he pulled out the emergency medical kit from the compartment under the dash.

"No drugs," Ryan said as he saw what Dr. Sid was doing.

"Captain?" Dr. Sid asked, looking at Gray as he got a shot of painkiller ready.

Gray looked at Ryan. Aki could sense the communication going on between them, even though neither man said a word. Finally Gray turned to Dr. Sid. "You heard the man."

Then Gray turned to Ryan. "We'll find the ship and be back for you."

"I'll stay with him," Jane said.

"Me, too," Neil said.

"Nobody's staying," Ryan said. "Just give me a gun." Aki watched as Ryan made the mistake of trying to move. He winced in pain.

Jane looked up at Gray.

"You got it," Gray said to Ryan. "Jane, give him a weapon."

Jane looked at Gray for a moment, clearly not liking the idea. Finally Gray said, "Just do it."

Jane moved around and yanked the big cannon off the back of the armored jeep. It was small enough for Ryan to handle in his position, yet had enough firepower to stop just about anything. She sat it up in

front of Ryan on a tripod and then lightly patted his
shoulder.

Less than thirty seconds later they were ready to
move.

"We'll be back for you, Sergeant," Gray said, looking
into the eyes of his wounded man. "You *hear* me?"

Aki knew, at that moment, without a doubt, that
Gray and the rest would risk their lives to return for
Ryan. She just hoped he would still be alive when they
did make it back. From the looks of his wounds, they
were going to have to make it fast.

"I hear you, Captain," Ryan said. Then he looked up
at Jane and Neil. "Now, get out of here. Go find something to cut me out of this mess."

Aki was impressed that Ryan managed to sound as
upbeat as he did.

"Let's move, people," Gray said, nodding to Ryan.

He turned and headed off toward the open hangar
area and the enclosed runway beyond.

Aki stepped into position behind him, not daring to
look back at Ryan. How Gray could do the things he
had to do was beyond her. Clearly it was what made
him a good leader.

And it was going to take a good leader to get them
all out of this dying city.

chapter 18

Gray made himself go slow and steady. He hated leaving Ryan like that, but rushing and getting the rest of them killed wouldn't help Ryan at all. They would make it back for him. And Ryan knew it.

Around them, the massive military hangar seemed to stretch into the distance. Smoke drifted through the building from a fire that engulfed what looked to be a crashed escape pod a few hundred meters away. A hole in the top of the building, where the pod had crashed through, was open to the sky. A runway-like area filled the center of the building, and dozens of aircraft and low-orbit transports, many clearly being worked on, lined both sides.

But they weren't looking for just any plane to take them out of here. Gray doubted if any of the ones he could see would even fly. They needed Aki's ship, the *Black Boa*.

In the distance down the runway the sound of gun-fire pierced through the smoke. Someone was fighting back, for some reason. Gray couldn't imagine why. More than likely they were just defending themselves. This city was lost. A good soldier knew when to fall back and regroup, and right now that was what he was hoping to do. Plus he and the Deep Eyes had to get Aki and Dr. Sid out of there, give their research a chance to work to stop this killing.

"There it is!" Aki shouted, pointing back in the direction they had come and across the runway.

Gray turned, half stunned. The drifting smoke had hidden the ship from them and they had almost walked past it.

They all turned and ran toward the ship. The closer they got, the more Gray could see of its situation. Some sort of towing tractor equipment was connected to the underside of the ship. The tractor had clearly been used to bring the *Black Boa* into the hangar.

The ship was parked off to one side of the runway, its tail in against the wall. It was sitting on what was called an airtray. An airtray was nothing more than a massive turntable, and at least a dozen ships besides the *Black Boa* were on this one. The airtray could be rotated so that any ship on the table was at the end of the runway and clear for take-off.

Gray stared at how the ship was sitting. He knew without a doubt that, before they could get the *Black Boa* out, they were going to have to get that airtray turned into the right position somehow.

Gray stopped and looked around as Aki went to a control panel on the landing strut of the ship. Behind him, though the smoke, he could see the control tower for this area of the hangar and airstrip. Someone was going to have to go up there and get the airtray turned and the ship into position.

He tried to look down the runway in the direction of the hangar doors. There was no telling if the doors at the far end of the interior runway were open or not, since he couldn't see them through the smoke. But Gray figured that if they had to, they could take their chances on smashing through the doors while in flight.

With a loud bang, the platform lift on the underside of the *Black Boa* descended and all of them got on, Jane and Neil watching for any sign of Phantoms. So far none could be seen, but Gray had no idea if they were still visible or not, and the smoke filling the hangar wasn't allowing for a long range of vision.

As the lift took them up into the *Black Boa*'s cargo bay, the lights came on. At a glance, Gray could tell the ship was well-stocked for any contingency.

"Hey, a quad-axle A.T.V.," Neil said, moving over to what was commonly referred to as a Quatro. "This is good."

A Quatro was a like a giant bubble with four legs. The legs could be used as stands, and also had heavy-duty wheels on them. It had massive remote-controlled arms that Gray knew could lift that jeep off Ryan easily.

"You're right," Dr. Sid said. "It could be used to retrieve Ryan and transport him here safely." As he talked, Dr. Sid reached down and pulled out two empty ovo-energy packs from the side of the Quatro. He held them up for Gray to see. "We need to replace these spent fuel cells."

"I think I saw some crates just down the line with ovo-pacs in them," Jane said.

Gray glanced around as everyone turned to him for instructions. "All right, Jane," he said, "check the hangar and find some ovo-pacs."

Jane nodded and headed for the lift.

Gray turned to Neil. "Get us ready for take-off."

"You got it," Neil said, heading for the cockpit of the ship.

"Aki, you and Dr. Sid get that Quatro prepped, on the lift, and ready to go with anything needed to get Ryan. I'm going to go to the tower to rotate the airtray. Let's do this thing and get the hell out of here."

"With pleasure," Dr. Sid said.

Aki looked at Gray as he moved to head down the lift. "Be careful."

"You, too," Gray said.

"Look what I found, Captain," Jane said as Gray reached the ground. She was standing two transports down the runway from the *Black Boa*, beside a large crate filled with rows of glowing green ovo-packs.

"Nice," he said as he ran up to her position. "Cover me, then get them into the ship."

He made the run across the open runway and into the base of the control tower without a problem. Thirty stairs later he was in the control room for the massive hangar.

It was a large space, with at least a dozen control stations. Four bodies lay slumped in different positions around the room, struck down by Phantoms before they could even move. Emergency power was still keeping the board lit and working. Gray just hoped emergency power also worked the airtray.

Gray eased the body of a young man with blond hair out of his chair and to the floor, then took his position at the board. Across the runway he could see Jane emerge from the *Black Boa* and go back for a second load of ovo-packs.

On the holographic images in front of him, Gray could see that the hangar door was open. Great. That was one problem solved. A couple of empty spaces on the holo-image showed where a few ships had made escapes.

Gray touched the holo-image of the *Black Boa,* but nothing seemed to happen. "Neil, can you hear me?"

Silence.

He flipped a few more switches, trying to remember what little he knew about these control-tower panels. It wasn't much. He'd only been in one of these rooms once before, and that was just for a social visit a few years back. But he was sure that the holo-images of the ships were control signals, including communications.

With one switch he managed to get the emergency flood lights lit over the runway. From across the way Jane gave him a thumbs-up signal.

Glancing down at the dead man beside him, Gray noticed the wireless headset the guy was wearing. He pulled it off the dead man's head and put it on, adjusting it to fit. Then he again touched the holo-image of the *Black Boa.* "Neil, do you read me?"

Neil's voice came back clear and crisp. "Loud and clear, Captain. This baby will fly itself when you're ready."

"Copy that," Gray said.

"Even got the flight path set," Neil said. "Autopilot on. You can trigger it from there if you have to."

"Great. You know anything about these airtray controls?" Gray asked.

"To your right," Neil said. "On the face of the side panel you should find the master switch and a big dial."

Gray glanced down at where Neil indicated. The controls were clear and simple. Gray set the rotation, then again touched the holographic image of the *Black Boa.* With a loud clang the airtray started to turn, moving at least six different ships with it at the same time.

"Beginning rotation," Gray said.

"Whoa!" Neil said. "Stop the airtray!"

Gray instantly did as Neil said, hitting the off switch. The airtray stopped with another loud clanging sound.

Neil studied the holo-images in front of him. "What's wrong?"

"We have a problem," Neil said. "I'm reading the impound tractor still attached to the prow of the ship."

Gray instantly understood why Neil had stopped the rotation. He stood so he could get a better view out the window. Below him, through the smoke, he could see that the impound tractor was not sitting on the airtray, but on the runway. If they had kept going, they would have dragged the *Black Boa* sideways and into the ship beside it on the airtray.

"Permission to go outside and detach the coupling," Neil said. "I can't seem to get it to work from here."

"Do it," Gray said. "And make sure you have Jane with you. And keep your communications headset on."

"Copy that," Neil said.

Gray leaned forward and tried to see if Ryan was still moving and all right. He couldn't tell. This entire situation was not looking good. One of his men was trapped under a jeep. Two scientists were working to get a Quatro running to save him, while his other two men prepared a ship so they could all escape into orbit.

There was nothing he could do at the moment but sit and wait for the signal from Neil that the rotation of the airtray could continue.

He looked around at the dead men, then out the control-tower window as Jane and Neil appeared on the *Black Boa* lift.

Gray could hear Jane's voice in the distance through Neil's headset.

"What's the problem?" Jane asked as they hit the ground.

"We're still locked down," Neil said, his voice coming through loud and clear to Gray. "We have to go uncouple the ship."

Through the smoke Gray could see Neil and Jane run to the impound tractor. Neil studied it for a moment while Jane stood guard.

From where Gray was standing he couldn't see any signs of Phantoms, but considering the dead men around him, they were not far away.

"There's the problem," Neil said. He mumbled something that Gray couldn't hear clearly, then said, "Naturally, the controls are locked. Can't ever be easy, can it?"

Gray had to agree with that. For some reason, nothing was coming easy.

"Jane," Neil said as he worked, his voice clear to Gray in the tower, "let me ask you something."

Gray could not hear Jane's response.

"You think we're going to get out of here alive?"

Gray watched as suddenly Jane took a step away from Neil and pointed her weapon down the runway.

"I mean," Neil said, going on talking while he worked, "I wonder if anybody has gotten out. You think anyone has made it so far?"

Gray followed the direction Jane was pointing. A number of Phantoms could be seen through the smoke, headed toward the *Black Boa.*

"You think," Neil went on, clearly ignoring the problems coming at them as he fought to release the ship from the towing tractor, "that this eighth-spirit stuff is gonna work against the Phantoms?"

Gray could not hear Jane say anything in return as she kept her weapon aimed at the Phantoms.

"I mean," Neil said, "what if it's all just a bunch of mumbo jumbo?"

There was a loud pop and Gray saw Neil jump back from the sparking machine. "Yeoww!" Neil said, shaking his hand. "You mind if we stop talking? I'm trying to concentrate here."

Gray could not hear if Jane said anything or not. He doubted she had, since her focus was on the Phantoms. They were not turning aside.

Finally, Jane could wait no longer. She opened up on the Phantoms, cutting them down as fast as they appeared.

"Neil," Gray said, "what's your status?"

"Almost there," Neil said.

Gray watched as Jane thinned out the Phantoms, one right after another. But for some reason they seemed to be getting worse, with more and more of them appearing.

"I want you two out of there," Gray said.

"We're fine, sir," Neil said. "Jane is negotiating with extreme prejudice."

Suddenly Neil clapped his hands together and grabbed his rifle. "We're good to go here, Captain," Neil said. "All clear."

He moved to a position beside Jane and opened up on the Phantoms.

Gray hit the start button on the airtray and the *Black Boa* and the other ships on the airtray jerked into motion. It was only going to take a few seconds and the ship would be ready to go.

Suddenly, before Gray could even shout a warning, a Phantom came up from right under Neil. It was as if Neil suddenly had tentacles sticking out of his chest and back and the top of his head.

"No!" Jane shouted, her wailing cry echoing throughout the hangar.

Neil, his blue spirit yanked out of his body, was instantly dead. He dropped to the ground as if every muscle in his body had turned to water.

Gray could not believe what had just happened.

Jane opened up on the Phantom that had killed Neil, firing through it until there was nothing left of it.

Suddenly she stopped and looked around her. A Meta was coming up out of the ground, surrounding her.

"Jane!" Gray shouted. "Get out of there! Run! Now!"

Jane ignored him. She continued to stand her

ground, dropping her weapon as an enigmatic smile played over her lips. She took a last look at Neil's body, then closed her eyes to accept the inevitable.

The tentacles of the Meta Phantom whipped around her, one slashing through her head before she even had a second to react.

Her blue life force flashed out of her body as she slumped beside Neil, clearly dead.

Gray looked out the window at the bodies of his two friends, and the Meta seemed to tower over the *Black Boa* as it rotated toward the end of the runway on the airtray. With a hard slam of his fist on the control board he started the autopilot of the *Black Boa* for liftoff and insertion into orbit.

He and the Deep Eyes were not going to make it out of here, but at least Aki and Dr. Sid would.

He picked up a chair and smashed it through the window. A moment later he had jumped through, landing on a patio eight meters below the control room.

"Come and get me!" he shouted at the monster Phantom, firing shot after shot into its huge mass, trying to turn it from the *Black Boa* and the woman he loved.

chapter 19

Aki felt her entire body go numb as she and Dr. Sid watched from the protected and barrier-shielded cargo hold as Neil and Jane were killed. The silence between them was so loud it almost hurt. She could not believe she had seen what had just happened out there. It wasn't possible. Not after all the fights and battles Jane and Neil had gone through.

But it *had* happened.

She knew it. There, on the screen, were Jane and Neil, lying beside each other on the concrete, dead.

The *Black Boa* was still moving on the airtray, rotating around until it was in position at the end of the runway. She knew Gray was in the control tower, but she didn't know if he was alive or dead.

Suddenly the control-tower window burst outward and Gray jumped to a patio area ten feet over the runway. Then he started firing and shouting at something

Aki couldn't see beside the *Black Boa.* More than likely it was the Phantom that had killed Neil and Jane.

It took her a moment to understand what he was doing. He was trying to save her and Dr. Sid by drawing the attention of the Phantom. But they were protected. They had up an ovo-energy shield. Didn't he know that? She was sure he did.

Something else was happening. She glanced around at the control panel on the wall of the cargo bay. It showed that the autopilot launch was set and counting down. The *Black Boa* was going to launch as soon as it got into position, leaving Gray and Ryan behind.

She couldn't allow that to happen.

She dropped the barrier shield that was up around her and Dr. Sid in the cargo area, then headed at a run for the passageway up to the cockpit. She had to get that autopilot off.

"Where are you going?" Dr. Sid asked as Aki stopped in the hallway to power up the barrier around him on her way out.

"Gray and Neil set the ship on autopilot," she said. "We're in countdown to liftoff."

"Oh," he said. He glanced at the view screen showing Gray firing and trying to draw the large Phantom's attention, then back at Aki.

Aki could tell he understood what she was doing. "Stay inside the protected shield area," she said, "no matter what happens. One of us has to get the information we have out of here."

He nodded and said nothing as she turned and headed up to the cockpit.

In the open lab, where she had spent so much time

searching for spirits from orbit, a phantom floated, moving from left to right as the ship rotated on the airtray. It was a small one and visible, as they all seemed to be after all the energy explosions in the city. She watched it carefully as she climbed up the ladder into the cockpit, making sure it suddenly didn't move after her. If one came through up there, she wouldn't stand a chance—there just wasn't enough room to get out of the way. And the cockpit wasn't shielded.

As she settled into the pilot's chair, she understood what Gray was firing at. She could see through the windows a Meta, so large that part of it extended above the roof of the hangar. It was not more than twenty meters to the right of the *Black Boa*, not seeming to get any closer or any farther away. However, just the whipping action of one of its massive tentacles could reach her at any moment.

She watched as Gray kept shouting words she couldn't hear at the Phantom and firing. Then suddenly from the left another stream of fire joined Gray's.

She leaned forward to see that Ryan was adding the jeep's old cannon power into the battle from his pinned position. The *Black Boa* had rotated right back to a position not more than a hundred meters from him.

From the looks of it, the heavy weapon wasn't making a difference on the Meta either. It wasn't moving away from the attack as Gray and Ryan kept pouring shot after shot into it.

She keyed in the communications link with Gray and then studied the ship's control panel. The *Black Boa* was within seconds of autopilot launch. If she couldn't stop the launch, they would be in orbit before she could do anything else.

Her fingers flew over the control board, working to lock out the signal from the control tower and take over launch control herself. She wasn't going to leave Gray and Ryan, not if she had anything to say about it.

Below she heard the rumble of the *Black Boa*'s engines kicking in.

"Stop, baby stop," she whispered, speeding up her efforts to override the tower control Gray and Neil had set.

"What are you doing?" Gray asked in her ear. She started. She had forgotten she had turned on the communication link. She didn't bother to answer him.

A moment later the *Black Boa* clicked into launch position and the airtray stopped.

"Autopilot launch," the computer said.

"Not if I can help it," Aki said.

"Aki!" Gray shouted in her ear. "Get back to the cargo bay. Now!"

Finally, just as the ship lifted off the ground, she managed to disengage the autopilot, taking over control and holding the ship level and hovering above the runway.

The Meta Phantom towered over her and the ship, blocking the runway. There was nowhere she could go. Gray and Ryan were going to have to win the fight out there, or none of them was escaping.

Now she understood what Gray had been trying to do, and why he wanted her back in the cargo bay. With the cargo hold shielded, it didn't matter if the ship flew through a Meta on the way out. Dr. Sid would survive.

She would have also, if she had remained down there with him.

But if the autopilot had launched the ship with her in the cockpit, she would be very, very dead.

She glanced down at the ship's control board again. Now she really understood why Gray was such a good soldier. He knew what needed to be done and focused on that. And what was really important now was getting Dr. Sid out of there and to safety, so that the information he had could be used to save everyone.

Gray knew that, and sitting there now, maybe moments from death, she understood it.

The Meta in front of her kept absorbing the fire from Ryan and Gray without moving.

She quickly programmed in the autopilot and set it to trigger the moment she took her hand from the panel. As long as she was alive, she would control the ship. But if something happened to her, the ship would take Dr. Sid to safety.

Outside the window Gray turned and killed a small Phantom coming up on him from the side, then went back to trying to move the Meta blocking the ship.

She could tell it just wasn't working.

Gray almost panicked when he saw Aki settle into the pilot's chair of the *Black Boa.* He could not believe that she had left the safety of the cargo hold and was in the cockpit. Yet there she was. No doubt she had Dr. Sid still protected in the cargo bay, but she would die if the ship went through the Meta.

He just hoped she realized he had the autopilot on and knew how to disengage it.

"Stop, baby stop," she whispered, her voice clear in his ear. So she *was* trying to disengage the autopilot.

"What are you doing?" Gray asked.

She didn't answer him, even though he knew she could hear him.

The airtray clicked into position and the *Black Boa* engines fired, lifting the ship from the ground in the normal autopilot launch sequence.

"Aki!" Gray shouted in her ear. "Get back to the cargo bay. Now!"

Again she didn't answer.

He fired into the Meta even harder and faster, trying to move it before it killed Aki along with Jane and Neil. If she didn't get that autopilot off, she was going to be dead in seconds.

Then, the ship stopped and hovered.

Clearly Aki had managed to free the ship.

He took a deep breath and let it out slowly. Now it was up to him and Ryan to clear the path for her and Dr. Sid to make it out of this death trap.

Even from over a hundred meters away, Gray could see the pain on Ryan's face as he fired the big cannon. Clearly the effort was costing him.

Suddenly Gray remembered the case of ovo-energy packs that Jane had found to power the barrier inside the cargo hold. It was tucked against one ship on the other side of the Meta. Maybe blowing them up would be enough of a distraction. But Gray doubted his gun would be powerful enough to set off the explosion they needed.

He signaled to Ryan that he should follow his shot.

Ryan nodded.

Then Gray took aim on the crate and fired.

He had been right. His rifle wasn't powerful enough to set off the reaction among the remaining ovo-packs.

But Ryan saw what he was doing and fired on the box, hitting it with the first shot.

The explosion rocked the _Black Boa_ in midair and sent Gray ducking for cover from flying debris.

The Meta turned and moved toward the energy surge, just as Gray hoped it would, clearing the way for the _Black Boa_ to take off.

But the explosion did other things as well. Suddenly more and more smaller Phantoms were coming in through the walls and down through the ceiling, also attracted by the new energy. It was like an invasion.

Gray opened fire on everything that came close to him, Ryan, or the ship.

Ryan was firing as well, taking them out with accurate shots from the large cannon. But Gray could see something Ryan couldn't see—a large, house-sized Phantom was coming up behind Ryan, coming at him through the truck.

Gray fired on it, hitting it but not stopping it.

Ryan knew what Gray was firing at, but really couldn't turn to help. He never saw his executioner coming.

The Phantom passed over Ryan and moved toward the source of energy from the burning ovo-packs.

Ryan's spirit shot up into the air and then vanished.

Gray fired and fired on the Phantom and killed it, before it had even finishing passing over Ryan. But it was far, far too late.

In his ear Gray heard Aki's voice. "Gray, do you read me?"

"You and Dr. Sid get out of here," Gray said, staring at Ryan's body. "Now!"

"No!" Aki said, her voice firm. "We're not leaving you."

"Everyone else is dead," Gray said, his voice almost horse. He didn't really want to hear those words out loud. Not now, not ever.

"I'm not leaving without you," Aki said.

"I'm sorry," Gray said, "but you don't have a choice. You have to get you and Dr. Sid out of here. Good-bye, Aki."

He kept firing on any Phantom that came close to him or got in front of Aki's ship.

"Sorry, Captain," Aki said. "You're with me whether you like it or not."

The *Black Boa* turned and moved toward him, hovering over him.

Suddenly the hatch opened over his head and the lift started to lower. He glanced around, firing on the smaller Phantoms that were coming in at him.

Suddenly, out of the floor of the deck area he was on, came three Phantoms. Spinning as he held the trigger down on his rifle, he killed all three of them before any of their tentacles could even brush against his leg.

The lift clanked to a stop beside him as he fired on two other Phantoms coming at him from the right.

"Gray!" Aki shouted into his ear. "Get on! Now!"

Gray glanced over at the Meta, who had turned and was slowly coming back toward them. He and Aki had very little time left to live if they stayed there.

He jumped onto the lift, firing at a smaller Phantom as he did.

"I'm on!" he shouted. "Go!"

Aki moved the *Black Boa* slowly forward as the lift pulled him upward. A flying Phantom came down out of the high ceiling, swooped in low, and came at him. He blew it out of the air.

Then the lift had him too close to the ship to safely fire. It clicked into place and he turned.

Dr. Sid was smiling at him.

"Glad to see you again, Captain," he said. His eyes were sad. It was clear that he had seen the deaths of the others on the view screen in the cargo bay.

"Hang on!" Aki's voice shouted through the ship's com system and in Gray's ear.

Gray moved over and stood against the back bulkhead, his rifle useless in his hand.

An instant later Aki fired both main thrusters, shoving Gray back against the bulkhead hard, banging his head against the metal.

"You all right?" Dr. Sid asked, the thrust twisting his words.

Gray said nothing. After today it would be a long, long time before he was all right.

On the view screen the ship managed to go past dozens of Phantoms and slip under the tentacles of another Meta, then flash out of the end of the massive hangar.

A moment later Aki tipped its nose toward space and all the engines kicked in.

Gray wasn't able to pull himself away from the bulkhead for the next two minutes of full thrust. It gave him time to think and remember Ryan, Jane, and Neil. He could not believe they were gone. Not after all they had been through before.

Three of his closest friends, and three of the best soldiers he had ever known were dead, left to rot on a hangar floor. They had given their lives to save Aki, Dr. Sid, and his life. He was going to make sure that sacrifice was worth it.

They would not be forgotten.

After the engine thrust shut down and released the *Black Boa* and its three passengers into the comfort of no gravity, Gray floated over and stared out the porthole at the Earth below. From this height everything looked so normal.

A moment later Aki come floating back toward them.

"Good work," Dr. Sid said, smiling at her.

He turned to face her and the expression of deep sadness on her face.

"Thanks," he said.

She nodded. "You would have done the same thing for me." She floated over to him and put her hand on his shoulder. "I'm sorry, Gray. I really am. They were great soldiers."

"And great people as well," Dr. Sid added, moving up toward the cockpit, leaving the two of them alone.

He nodded and put his head on her shoulder, closing his eyes and letting the soft feel of her against him take some of the pain.

"I wish I could believe," he said after a moment, "that they were in a better place."

"Maybe Dr. Sid and I can prove it to you some day," Aki said, her voice soft and comforting.

"I hope so," Gray said.

For the longest time he allowed himself to just float there in her arms, remembering the three who had given their lives to save them.

Then slowly he looked up at her. The understanding and pain were clear in her eyes. Gently, she kissed him.

chapter 20

General Hein sat strapped in a chair behind his desk, the seat belt keeping him from floating in the zero gravity. He had ordered the shuttle to hold its position in orbit and not move until he gave the order. Then he had locked himself in his room. That had been two hours ago.

Two long hours of getting ready to do what he knew needed to be done.

On his desk a small screen showed an aerial image of what had been Barrier City New York. Using the screens on the satellite visuals, he could see the Phantoms, roaming the streets and moving through the buildings of the now-dead city. He could even see the human bodies scattered in the streets and on the rooftops. A dozen fires still raged, getting larger instead of smaller, since there was no one left alive down there to contain them.

Yet just last night that city had been alive and full of millions of humans, not Phantoms.

It had been full of people he had killed.

He studied the image for another moment, then clicked off the screen. He reached down and un-snapped his side arm from its holster. He had gotten the weapon twenty years before, as a present from his father when he made captain. He had carried it every day since.

He studied it like an old friend. The metal shone, the handle perfectly polished, as always. It seemed that he and this old friend were going to have one final talk be-fore deciding to move on.

He clicked it open to make sure it was loaded, then made sure a shell was in the chamber and clicked the hammer back.

Millions of deaths.

He had caused millions of deaths. This would only be one more.

No one would even notice.

He put the gun to his temple, then changed his mind and put the barrel of it in his mouth. Less chance of missing that way.

The metal was cold, and the taste metallic and bitter.

That was perfect for him. He need to taste his death, to make sure it was going to happen.

He took a pillow he had tucked under the side of his chair to keep it from floating away and put it against the back of his head. His brain, skull, and the pillow would slow the bullet down enough that it wouldn't cause too much damage to the shuttle. The men on board this shuttle were good men. No point in killing even more good people when all he wanted to do was kill himself.

He twisted the gun in his hand while holding the pillow against the back of his head. It scraped on his tongue as the images of the people dying on that rooftop filled his mind.

The memory of Major Elliot clutching his chest replaced the other memories. Elliot had been a decent soldier. Not smart, just decent. A loyal man who followed orders. He hadn't deserved to die like that.

None of them had deserved to die.

Hein knew he had killed a lot of good people today. All he had to do was pull the trigger and he would never have to think about it again.

The barrel of the gun banged against his upper teeth.

Pull it!

Just pull the trigger.

His body tensed.

Pull it!

Now!

His finger didn't move on the trigger. He could see his hand holding the gun, and the top of the barrel. His hand was starting to shake, the gun moving in his mouth.

Pull it, you coward!

His finger didn't move. Only his body tensed.

He stared at his hand, the metal hard in his mouth.

Finally, disgusted, he pulled the gun from his mouth and let the pillow float away in the zero gravity. He had killed millions, and now he was too much of a coward to even kill one more. How stupid was that?

He closed his eyes and leaned back in his chair. He didn't want to go on, live one more hour, with the thought of those deaths on his conscience. No one could live like that.

But why couldn't he just kill himself and be done with it?

What was stopping him?

The image of a Phantom moving over the top of a man on the rooftop flashed into his head.

Then he knew the answer.

Of course!

He shouldn't really be killing himself, he should be going after the true cause of all the deaths: the Phantoms. Just as he couldn't actually kill himself, he hadn't actually killed anyone directly. Granted, he had let the Phantoms into the city, but everyone who knew that was dead.

Besides, the Phantoms would have gotten in at some point anyway.

The Phantoms had killed every one of those people. And his wife and daughter. And they would kill many more if he didn't stop them.

Had he forgotten that?

He had the means of killing them in return, of wiping them from the face of the planet.

He put his gun back in its holster, sat up, and took a deep breath. Then he tapped the communications button on his desk.

"Yes, sir?" the pilot said.

"Zeus cannon station," he said. "How long until we can reach it?"

"Ninety minutes," the pilot said.

"Set a course," he said. "And get us there as fast as you can."

He clicked off the communications link and sat back in his chair. He would avenge all the deaths tonight by wiping the Phantoms from existence, if it was the last thing he ever did.

Aki had tried to help Gray for the first hour after they had reached orbit. She had just held him, the two of them floating in the middle of the cargo bay.

Gray had said nothing and done nothing, never mentioning the three who had died for them. It seemed that just the two of them floating together had been enough. Maybe later they would be able to talk about Jane and Ryan and Neil. But not yet. The grief was too much, too soon.

Dr. Sid had left the cargo bay right after the *Black Boa* reached orbit, moving up to the lab, and when Aki finally let Gray have a few minutes alone, she found that Dr. Sid was already working in the lab to find the next spirit.

As she floated into the room, he flipped on the holographic image of the Phantom spirit, its wave form flowing upward like spiraling red smoke from the center of the lab table.

Then, as Aki pulled herself around into an upright position and watched, Dr. Sid brought up the wave with the seven spirits they had collected. The two looked almost exactly the same.

As Aki compared the two waves, Dr. Sid moved the holograms closer and closer until they covered each other. Suddenly all that was left was the one spirit shape they were missing. The eighth spirit.

Aki knew they were so close. After all this time, all they needed was one more.

"I started the search pattern," Dr. Sid said.

"Same parameters as last time?" Aki remembered that it had taken them less than a day to find the seventh spirit in the wasteland. She hoped they could find this one as fast.

Dr. Sid shook his head. "No, this time I included areas we had previously overlooked, just to be safe. Who knows when we're going to get another chance, after what happened."

Aki nodded. She had no doubt that General Hein would have them arrested again the first chance he got. But expanding the search parameters had problems. "Isn't that going to make the search harder, and more time-consuming?"

"No, it won't," he said. "We have such an exact reading on what the last spirit is shaped like, we can increase the size of each grid, thus making it easy to expand the search. And more logical."

"If you say so," she said. "So where do we stand with—"

Suddenly the sound of beeping filled the lab. She spun so hard she lost her grip for a moment on the lab table and floated up toward the ceiling.

Dr. Sid seemed stunned as well. That was the signal that they had found the last spirit.

Gray floated in from the hallway as Aki pushed herself down beside Dr. Sid. Together they stared at the computer screen, looking at the results of the search.

"What's all the beeping mean?" Gray asked.

"We found it," Aki said, smiling at him.

"The eighth spirit?"

"A positive match," Dr. Sid said.

Then Aki looked at the exact location where the green light was blinking on the hologram image of the surface of the planet. "That can't be."

Her stomach twisted, and she could feel the sweat on her hands. The light showed the eighth spirit was in the Phantom crater.

Gray moved up and studied the map as well. Then he laughed, as if the readings were a joke. "I've got to say, that's a strange place to find the eighth spirit."

Dr. Sid nodded, going over the sensor readings as he spoke, double-checking everything. "Yes, really quite astonishing."

Aki watched as Dr. Sid inserted the last piece, the basic image of the last spirit he had scanned from below, into the swirling hologram image they had been trying to build.

A perfect match. The computers were right. The eighth spirit was down there in the crater, there was no doubt.

"That's it," Aki said, trying to catch her breath at finally having the last spirit that would save her, and maybe the entire human race.

"Can't be," Gray said. "Nothing could survive in that impact crater except Phantoms."

"Precisely," Dr. Sid replied.

Aki looked at him, stunned and amazed at he had just said. "You want to explain that?"

He smiled. "What we have here is clear evidence that the eighth spirit is a Phantom spirit."

Aki felt her entire body go numb. It couldn't be possible. How could a Phantom spirit be the key to saving her from a Phantom infestation?

"I can't explain it at the moment," Dr. Sid said, staring at the image of the completed spirits spiraling in front of him, "but I'm sure that once we get down there, we'll understand."

"Wait," Gray said, holding up his hand. "Doctor, that's a one-way trip you're talking about there."

Dr. Sid looked at Gray and just smiled.

Aki knew that look. It was one he used to give his students when he was explaining something simple.

"I expected that was how you would evaluate our chances," Dr. Sid replied.

"Well?" Gray asked, "Am I wrong?"

"Doctor?" Aki asked, wanting to know the same answer. "It is a one-way trip, isn't it?"

"Yes, yes, I'm afraid it just might be." He said that without looking at either one of them. Then he looked up at Aki, holding her gaze. "I agree that we probably won't live long enough to *extract* the eighth spirit from the crater."

"So what would be the point?" Gray asked. "Why should we even try it?"

"Because," he said, "we don't need to extract the eighth and final spirit."

"I see," Aki said. She was finally starting to understand what the doctor was talking about.

"You want to clue me in then?" Gray asked, his patience clearly pushed to its limits.

"If we can't bring the final spirit here," Aki said, pointing to the lab, "then we go there and complete the wave inside the crater."

"Exactly," Dr. Sid said.

"And how do we do that?" Gray asked, looking first at her and then at Dr. Sid. "Exactly?"

"I can construct a device that would attach to Aki's chestplate," he said, "to gather the eight spirits and then . . ."

Dr. Sid stopped and didn't look as if he was going to continue as he turned his attention back to the computer screen and the readouts pouring in from the scans.

Aki glanced at the puzzled frown on Gray's face, then back at her mentor. She had no idea exactly what would happen at the point when all eight spirits were together and came in contact with a Phantom wave. She doubted Dr. Sid did, either. They both had theories, but it was nothing more than that, since they had not yet gotten all eight spirits to run tests with.

"And then what, Doctor?" Gray asked.

Dr. Sid just shrugged. "And then we wait and see what happens."

"You're kidding?" Gray asked. "That's your plan? We wait and see what happens?"

"Yes," Dr. Sid said, looking at Gray. "That is *exactly* what we do."

Gray looked at her, then at the hologram spiraling above the table, then at Dr. Sid. "Oh, good. Well, I've got my plan. How about we keep scanning the surface from orbit, and maybe we'll find a compatible spirit somewhere else?"

Aki looked at Gray, then turned to Dr. Sid. She knew what had to be done.

"Aki?" Gray asked. "Tell me you're not thinking of doing this? Please?"

Aki placed her hand inside the swirling hologram and looked first at Dr. Sid, then at Gray. "I say we go in."

Gray just shook his head. "I was afraid that would be your answer."

She just smiled.

"Well," he said, "if you two are insisting on this mission, at least let me try to figure out a way to get us out."

"Sounds fine to me," Aki said, "but we don't have much time, remember."

"I won't take much time," he said. "How long until you are ready, Dr. Sid?"

"Four hours."

"Then I'll be ready on my end in four hours as well," Gray said.

Aki watched him turn and push himself back down into the cargo hold.

Dr. Sid patted her hand. "Don't worry," he said. "If anyone can get us in and out of the crater alive, it's your boyfriend, there. Captain Edwards has done amazing things so far."

"I hope he can pull off one more," she said.

But honestly, she doubted if any of them would come out of that crater alive. But if things worked the way she and Dr. Sid hoped, their three lives would be the last three lives ever taken by a Phantom.

And that would be worth dying for.

chapter 21

The airlock hissed open in front of General Hein and he floated into the Zeus space station, not really enjoying the feeling of pulling himself along. Zero g was not something he liked, but at least he was at the station.

Two soldiers secured against the walls on either side of the airlock snapped to attention as he boarded. He returned their salute, but said nothing. Right now he had work to do if he was going to destroy the cause of all those deaths in New York.

The Zeus station main control room was large. There were a dozen stations on different levels around the room, and when he entered, each station except the main one was manned. Major Sinn was the man in command of the station when he wasn't here, and right now Major Sinn was floating in a standing position to one side, saluting, as did every other man in the command area.

"Return to your posts," Hein said, snapping off a salute and kicking himself toward the command chair.

With a quick motion he was in the chair and had the belt on, holding him down. At least that gave him a feeling of normal gravity.

"Happy to see you made it out of New York," Major Sinn said.

"Happy to have made it," Hein said, keying in the command to call the Council. He had asked en route that they be ready for his call when he reached the station, and they had agreed.

A hologram flickered into being in front of him. It was a three-dimensional representation of the secondary council chamber in the Houston barrier city. All the Council members were present. The details were so good that it seemed that the Council members were only inches tall and actually right in the room.

"What caused the New York barrier to fail?" Councilwoman Hee asked without a word of greeting.

Hein had expected such an attack, and he had spent the last few hours getting ready for it. "I was afraid," he said, shaking his head in sadness, "that it was only a matter of time before the Phantoms developed an immunity to our barriers. I actually saw Phantoms swimming in the ovo-energy pipes leading from the main energy station."

The Council sat there in stunned silence. He knew exactly what they were thinking. If New York could fall, then so could every other barrier city in the world. The human race would be wiped out. And that was exactly what he wanted them to think.

"But I am relieved to see that you, Councilwoman

Hee, and the rest of the Council, were able to evacuate to Houston without incident."

Hein waited as the tiny holographic images of the council shifted in front of him, taking in the fact of the Phantoms developing an immunity to the barrier energy.

Finally Councilwoman Hee spoke again, talking slowly, as if she were forcing herself to say things she did not want to say. "It was a terrible loss we suffered yesterday in New York."

General Hein nodded, saying nothing. It was better that he didn't speak.

Councilwoman Hee went on. "The Council has reconsidered your proposal to fire the Zeus cannon."

Hein could barely contain himself, and didn't trust himself at that moment to utter a full sentence without showing emotion. So instead, he said softly, "I see."

"We are transmitting the access codes to the Zeus cannon now," the councilwoman said. She then turned to an aide standing behind her and nodded.

The computer beside Hein beeped softly. He looked at the screen, watching as the computer verified the security information, then put the six-number code on the screen.

"I have it," he said.

Councilwoman Hee, her small holographic image looking even smaller and more tired, nodded. "General," she said, "best of luck to us all."

The Council then cut the communication.

He wanted to fly into the air with joy, but instead he just sat there. His plan had worked—maybe not perfectly, but it had worked. Now it was time to clean the planet of the enemy, and the best place to start was their home.

He stood and turned to Major Sinn. "Prepare to fire the cannon."

Major Sinn smiled and snapped off a salute. "Yes, sir!"

He turned and said to the officer at the weapons station. "You heard the general. Prepare to fire the cannon."

"The target, sir?" the officer asked, also smiling.

General Hein knew that this day was the day every soldier on this station had worked so hard to attain. Finally they were going into action, and they all believed, as he did, that they would save the world with this weapon.

"The Phantom crater."

His fingers ran over the board in front of him, and on the main viewscreen the Phantom crater appeared.

"Yes, sir!" the officer said.

"Finally," Major Sinn said, floating to a position beside General Hein.

Hein didn't take his gaze from the image of the crater. Yes, finally. The cost had been high, but without a doubt, saving the human race and winning this war would be worth it.

Aki leveled the *Black Boa* out over the impact crater. It was a massive scar, ripped into the Earth. When it had hit the planet, years before Aki had been born, millions had died in the earthquakes and tidal waves that immediately followed the collision, and it had caused years of cold temperatures from all the dust and debris tossed into the air.

But those millions of deaths were nothing compared to the deaths that came as the Phantoms slowly spread out from the crater over the years that followed, killing as they went. It was amazing that the human race still existed, let alone could fight back against the Phantoms.

She looked down into the crater at the remains of the meteor, the dream flashing into her mind. There, in that crater—she was sure—was the hunk of planet she had seen blown into space in her dream.

She checked where the *Black Boa* was hovering. A few hundred meters below was the top rim of the crater. The crater itself was a good kilometer across and hundreds of meters deep.

"How's this?" she asked into the communications link.

"Going to have to do," Gray said. "We don't dare go any lower. This will be fine as long as we're right over the meteor."

"We are," Aki said and set the controls to keep the ship hovering there for as long as they needed it to.

Then she got up and moved into the lab. Dr. Sid was studying the images of the Phantoms in the crater. He glanced up at her. "There are so many of them."

"Didn't need to hear that," she said. "Just find the right one." She patted him on the shoulder and moved on down toward the cargo bay.

Gray was making the final adjustments on the Quatro. He had decided they were going to use it as a base, staying inside it as they were lowered into the crater. He was convinced that the barrier shield around the Quatro would last for hours before it needed new fuel cells. He had also stocked it with just about every weapon he could fit inside, and had even managed to mount a small cannon on the outside. He was a soldier, and he told Aki that he wasn't walking into the enemy camp without being fully armed.

She had agreed, and was silently glad he was doing what he was doing.

"Ready?" he asked as she entered the cargo hold.

"As I'll ever be," she said.

"We can find another way, you know."

She shook her head. "This is the best way."

"If you say so." He indicated she should get inside the Quatro, then he followed, snapping the hatch down. The Quatro was big enough inside for both of them to sit beside each other and stare out the large front window. The controls and sensory equipment were showing active, with at least a half dozen small holograms on the panel and another dozen control holograms around them.

The feel of his shoulder against hers gave her confidence. No matter what happened, they would be together.

Aki checked out what Gray had done over the last few hours to the Quatro. It was now really the ultimate in all-terrain vehicles. It had wheels and tracks. It had lift jets that could power it twenty meters into the air and then land it safely, and it was completely shielded from the Phantoms. It also had claw arms for lifting and ripping anything from hard metal to entire trees. Now, with Gray's help, it had enough firepower to defend itself against an army.

"Powering the shield," Aki said, her hands moving over the control panel in front of her.

The barrier shield snapped on around them, giving everything they could see through the bubble a faint, swirling, golden tint.

"Starting descent," Gray said.

The Quatro rocked as the lift picked it up and moved it out over the open cargo bay door. They were going down on the end of a cable. That also had been Gray's idea. When she was worried about that long a cable being strong enough, he had laughed. He had said it would pull the *Black Boa* out of the sky before it would break.

Gray replaced the main window with a scan of what they were lowering themselves into. Never in all her life had she seen anything so horrifying in its emptiness.

Below them, a twisted rock tip of the meteor stuck into the air. She knew, from their readings in orbit, that there had to be Phantoms there. Millions of them, but all she could see was the barren insides of the impact crater.

Gray glanced over at Aki. "You sure about this?"

"No," she said, imagining the swarming Phantoms she couldn't see coming closer and closer as they were slowly lowered into the crater.

"Dr. Sid," Gray said into the com link with the *Black Boa*, "do you have our target in sight?"

"There are so many of them."

Now she was glad she couldn't see them. She really didn't want to understand this close why he kept saying that.

"Wait!" Dr. Sid shouted, his voice echoing in the

small space inside the Quatro. "Yes, I'm tracking the eighth spirit, moving along the crater's surface."

On the screen on the Quatro's control panel, the Phantom target was highlighted by Dr. Sid. It seemed, as far as Aki could tell, to be pretty much right below them.

"Let's take a closer look," Gray said.

The next moment a Meta Phantom tentacle pounded into the Quatro's screens and bounced off. Golden sparks flew and the lights inside dimmed slightly. Aki knew, without a doubt, that if the screens hadn't held, they would now both be dead.

The lower they went, the more invisible Phantoms bumped and ran into the screen. It flared, it sparked, but it held. She had no idea how long the Quatro's screens would last. With luck, just long enough to do the job and get out.

Without luck, just long enough to do the job.

chapter 22

General Hein leaned back in his command chair and listened to the well-run control room as it prepared to attack the enemy. He had sat in this very chair during many trial runs, hungry for the time when this master weapon would be allowed to fire for real. Today was the day.

On the main screen was the image of the impact crater. And in that crater were millions of Phantoms. Soon they would all be dead.

"Ready to fire in three minutes," Major Sinn announced from where he stood at the secondary control board. General Hein had the master board in front of him, but at the moment he was content to let the major do the work.

"Ovo-packs at maximum," one soldier said from a station near the back of the room. "Transferring plasma flow to auto."

"Confirmed," Major Sinn replied. "Plasma flow on auto."

"Counter-thrusters are engaged," another soldier said.

General Hein leaned forward and checked that on his main board. The counter-thrusters had to fire, or the power of the weapon would drive the entire station up and out of orbit. He could see that all the counter-thrusters were green and set to go.

"Lox flow status is green," another soldier said.

"Confirmed," Major Sinn answered.

All of these responses were like presents to a child on Christmas. He loved and treasured every one of them. It was all moving so—

An alarm broke the perfect order of the room, blaring a warning so loud that he came up out of his chair.

"We have a ship over the impact site, sir," a soldier said from the tactical station to Hein's right.

"What?" General Hein said, staring at the young soldier for a moment. Then he dropped back into his seat and pulled the information up on his own board.

It took him a moment to understand what he was looking at. But when he did, he laughed—not because it was funny, but with the irony of it all. The ship was the *Black Boa*. That was Dr. Ross's ship, and clearly they were trying something with their crazy theory, since a shielded Quatro was dangling from a cable underneath it.

"Turn off that alarm," he said.

He stared at the image of the ship as the alarm went silent.

Dr. Ross would die with her beloved Phantoms. What a wonderful end. Perfectly fitting.

"One minute to firing," one soldier said.

"What do we do about the ship?" Major Sinn asked. "You want us to warn them off?"

"No, we fire as planned," General Hein said, sitting back in his chair, trying not to laugh.

"Sir?" Major Sinn asked.

"That ship is just a traitor's ship, under the influence of the enemy. I'm familiar with it. We continue the countdown. We'll just take them all out at once. A fitting end to a traitor, don't you think?"

"Yes, sir," the major said.

Hein sat and stared at the screen. The *Black Boa* was now clearly visible against the background of the Phantom-infested crater. It would soon no longer exist.

"Target locked," Major Sinn reported. "We are ready to fire on your order."

General Hein savored the moment for just one second, then he said, "Fire!"

Aki sat beside Gray as the Quatro swung slightly on the end of the cable. Their shoulders were pressed together, and Aki liked the closeness of it. Having him there gave her strength and comfort. Around them the golden swirling of the shield protected them from all the unseen Phantoms she knew filled the emptiness of the impact crater. She just couldn't see them with her naked eye.

Dr. Sid's voice crackled over the com link, clearly more excited than Aki had heard him be in years. "It's the one all right. The wavelength is a perfect match."

Aki stared at the Phantom Dr. Sid had found, now

on their screen. It was a dot moving slowly toward them across the crater floor. It was small, and from what she could tell from her sensor readings, looked to have at least ten legs or tentacles, all working in unison. It couldn't be more than fifty meters away.

"We called those kind *bugs*," Gray said. "They're fast and very nasty."

"What Phantom *isn't* nasty?" Aki asked.

"Point well made," he said. "Any idea what you are going to do now?"

Aki looked at him. He wasn't going to like her answer.

Suddenly everything around them went pure white.

Aki instantly put an arm up over her eyes to shield them, and the Quatro snapped down a dozen light filters even faster.

The Quatro was then smashed sideways and into the cliff wall, throwing Gray and Aki together on the small floor. Aki felt her arm bend back, but not break. And her breath was knocked out of her.

The burst lasted for at least a second, then stopped.

"You all right?" Gray asked as he untangled his legs from hers and they helped each other back to their seats.

"I think so," she said. She tested her arm and shoulder. It hurt, but not bad enough to need anything. If she lived through this, she was going to be very sore tomorrow.

Gray had a small cut on his cheek, but he looked to be fine as well.

On the screen Aki could not believe what she was seeing. The Quatro had managed to stay on the cable, but it was swinging wildly now, out over the crater and then back toward the cliff.

Gray frantically worked the small thrusters to stop

the movement. They were just about to plow into the rocks again when somehow he managed to slow the swing and stabilize them.

Below them, the Phantom crater had changed. The rough surface of the impact zone, where the tip of the meteor had been sticking up into the air, was now blasted even deeper into the Earth. And large cracks had opened up, twisting through the dirt like lightening bolts.

Aki pointed at the meteor. At least half of it had been buried before, but was now showing. And it, too, was splintered with cracks.

She checked her screens. An area that had been an anthill full of Phantoms now read deserted and lifeless.

"What happened?" Aki asked.

Gray glanced up from his board to look at the crater. "That was the Zeus cannon. They're firing at the crater."

Aki was stunned. "Didn't they see us down here?"

"I don't think General Hein would care," Gray said, "do you?"

She had to admit she knew he would take any opportunity to get rid of her and Dr. Sid. And since the Council had clearly given him permission to fire the Zeus cannon, by being here they were giving him his chance.

"Aki?" Dr. Sid's voice broke into the Quatro. "Gray? Are you all right?"

Aki was glad Dr. Sid was still there.

"A little shaken," Gray said. "Stand by."

Suddenly Aki realized what she was seeing in front of her. The Phantoms inside the crater were gone. And the eighth spirit blip was not on her screen, as it had been a moment before. Maybe they had all gone into hiding.

"Dr. Sid," she said, "can you track the eighth spirit?"

There was a long few seconds of silence, then Dr. Sid's voice came back, weak and tired-sounding. "The eighth spirit has been destroyed."

Aki looked out at the now-empty meteor crater in stunned silence. They had been so close. The spirit had been within fifty meters of her.

Now it was gone. Dead.

"What are we going to do now?" she asked.

Gray shook his head. "Nothing. This mission is over. We have to get out of here."

"And go where?" Aki asked. As far as she could see, there was no hope left.

Gray just shrugged and kept working. "Anywhere is better than the home base of a billion Phantoms."

He pointed out on the crater floor. As she watched, Phantoms, thousands of them, swarmed up out of the ground and from the sides of the meteor. The difference was now she could see them through the shielding with her naked eye. Somehow, the firing of the Zeus cannon had made them visible.

She had never seen anything like it. Where were they coming from? What was under there?

The Phantoms spread out over the bottom of the crater like kids over a playground at recess. And a large number of them were headed right at them.

"I sure hope the shield will hold," Aki said, looking at the golden glow surrounding them.

Gray nodded as he checked the control panel. "For the moment it will. But I can't tell you for how long."

chapter 23

General Hein was stunned that Dr. Ross's ship and the Quatro hanging under it had somehow survived the first shot of the Zeus cannon. The ship had been just enough off-center from the main force of the Zeus cannon, or it clearly never would have.

Of course, Dr. Ross and her friends might not be alive in there. There was just no telling what that much energy did to a human. It was designed to kill Phantoms.

As he watched, the Quatro stabilized itself. Now there was no doubt Dr. Ross had survived.

"One minute and ten seconds to second firing," Major Sinn reported. "All systems are go and stable. Awaiting your permission to continue."

"Fire when ready," he said. "And target that meteor directly. Let's take out the enemy's home base completely. They're under that rock somewhere. All we have to do is dig them out."

"Understood," Major Sinn replied. "Target the meteor."

"Targeting, sir," another soldier at tactical replied.

General Hein sat back in his chair, his hands folded on his lap. This had started out to be the worst day of his life. It was turning into a great day for all of humanity.

Around him the soldiers called out their reports as the next shot got closer and closer.

"Incoming!" Dr. Sid shouted through the communications link.

Gray instantly reached over and pulled Aki down out of the window. They had just enough time to get on the floor and brace themselves against each other and the equipment before the blast hit.

Again, everything lit up a bright white. Gray could feel the Quatro swing on the end of the cable, and he held Aki tight in his grasp. He was sure they were in for another pounding.

And he wasn't disappointed.

The Quatro smashed into the wall of the crater, spinning them like they were a child's toy. Gray felt the skin on his leg break open against one machine. Blood dripped down his leg.

The impact passed quickly as the Quatro swung back out over the crater. He checked to make sure nothing on his leg was broken. It wasn't. Otherwise, he was okay. Then he climbed back into his chair and quickly got them stabilized.

Then he turned to see if Aki was all right. She was holding her arm and rubbing her shoulder, but she claimed no problems. It was clear that, even with the protection of the Quatro, they couldn't take much more of this kind of beating. He had to get them out of there and quickly.

"Oh, my," Aki said, staring out the window.

The last blast of the Zeus cannon had smashed the meteor even more, breaking it apart like an eggshell. As they watched, a mass of Phantom tissue seemed to bubble from the cracks in the rock, rolling outward and filling the area where the meteor had been before.

It clearly was a Phantom, Gray had no doubt. But a Phantom so big, so dense, it could have covered all of the old New York Manhattan area, and had bulk left over.

"Did the meteor just hatch?" he asked.

"It's the Phantom Gaia," Aki said, her voice almost reverent in nature.

"You're kidding?" Gray said, staring at the massive, writhing behemoth that was flowing outward and upward, slowly filling the crater. *That* was a god? An alien god?

Suddenly, for the first time, he actually believed Aki when she said everything came and returned to Gaia. When he had been with Aki, in her dream, this monster was what he saw flowing up and into the hunk of planet being blown out into space. Now he understood what she had been talking about. Earth had a Gaia, and that alien planet had had a Gaia. And right now, he was looking at it.

As he watched, Phantoms of all sizes started pouring off the massive creature, separating from it like water shaking from skin. This was why when they killed a

Phantom, another took its place. It was happening right now, right in front of their faces.

Thousands of Phantoms, large and small, in all the sizes and shapes Gray was familiar with, were being reborn from the monster Phantom, pouring off and out of it.

"I think," Aki said, turning to him, "that if you are going to get us out of here, now would be a good time."

She was right. Gray instantly jumped to work. But the moment he tried to start the Quatro back upward, he knew they were in trouble. The cable connection to the Quatro had been smashed twice into the rocks. The moment he started the retraction engine, it broke free.

For an instant they were weightless as the fall started, like an elevator dropping too fast.

Gray quickly fired the Quatro thrusters, letting the autosystems of the vehicle control their decent.

"Oh, no," Aki said as the walls of the giant Phantom loomed up over them. More and more smaller Phantoms were pouring off of it, replacing the ones killed before.

Gray ignored everything.

He had to focus on getting them down. More than likely they were going to be killed by Phantoms, but at least that would be better than being smashed on the rocks below.

Somehow, just as the fuel was about to run out for the small machine, he lodged the Quatro into some massive boulders near one wall of the crater. For the moment, the monster Phantom had not reached that far, but all the other smaller Phantoms pouring off it had. And they were banging into the Quatro's shield one after another, making it spark and light up.

Then, just when Gray didn't think anything could get any worse, the Zeus cannon fired again, knocking them to the floor for the third time.

After the white light had cleared, Gray helped Aki up again. The Quatro had stayed wedged in the rocks, and most of the smaller Phantoms were gone from the crater. The crater floor itself was being shattered. Massive cracks were everywhere.

But the big alien Gaia was still there, flowing and pulsating in all its ugly glory.

"The Zeus cannon doesn't seem to hurt it," Aki said.

From where Gray stood, feeling like he was almost under the thing, she was right. The mother of all Phantoms seemed to be getting stronger, not weaker.

chapter 24

General Hein looked at the massive Phantom on the screen. The Zeus weapon had killed all the smaller Phantoms for miles around, and exposed this big one. But a second, direct shot from the Zeus cannon hadn't seemed to stop it or destroy it. And he didn't like the thought of that at all.

"Do you have a reading as to exactly what that thing is?" he asked, turning around to look at Major Sinn.

"I don't, sir," he said.

"Well, find out!" he shouted. "And start the next firing sequence. Another shot might just do the trick."

"Yes, sir," the major said.

Hein turned back to the screen to watch. Thousands of smaller Phantoms were pouring off the bigger one, spreading out over the floor of the crater like ants after their nest had been stepped on. Well, he was going to step on it again and again until none of them came out.

"Sir, incoming message."

He glanced at his board and realized it was Dr. Ross. She was clearly in the Quatro, which had broken free of the *Black Boa* and now rested in some rocks near one wall. The *Black Boa* had managed to almost crash-land a short distance from the crater, safely out of the line of fire.

Behind her he could see Captain Edwards. Amazing they had made it out of the city alive.

He smiled to himself. This was going to be interesting. He must hear what she had to say. He punched the receive button.

"General Hein," Dr. Ross said, her voice breathless, "you have to cease fire immediately."

"Oh, I do? And why would that be?"

"What you are looking at in the crater is the living spirit of an alien's homeworld. Their planet was destroyed, and part of it landed here. This is not an invasion, and never has been."

He laughed. "I see, Dr. Ross. What have we been fighting all this time? Ghosts?"

The men around him laughed at his joke.

"Yes," Dr. Ross said.

That silenced the control room.

"They are spirits, confused and lost and angry," she said.

He stared at her. She clearly believed what she was saying, of that there was no doubt.

"So these ghosts, as you call them, are coming out of this Gaia thing Dr. Sid sold the council on, is that right?"

"General Hein, you have to listen."

"Alien Gaia, Earth Gaia," Hein said, shaking his head. "Doctor, even if I believed such nonsense, the fact remains that the Earth is under attack from an aggressor who must be destroyed at all costs."

"The cost may be the entire planet, sir," she said, her gaze burning from the hologram image. "Firing at the alien Gaia will only make it stronger."

"Well," Hein said, laughing at her insane idea, "since you are under the alien's influence, I will take your protest to mean that we are in fact pursuing the correct course of action."

"I am not controlled by the aliens!"

"I suggest," he said, "that you take your last few minutes and prepare to meet your Gaia."

He clicked off the connection and then turned to Major Sinn. "Continue to fire until the invader has been destroyed. Step up the pace. I want one shot every two minutes from now on."

"Yes, sir," the major said.

He stared at the image of the massive alien filling the crater. Nothing could stand up against the might of the Zeus cannon. And now that he had dug this creature out of its hiding place and into the light, he would blast it into dust.

Gray squeezed her shoulder. "I don't think he believed a word you said."

Aki wanted to smash something, especially the smirk off the general's face, but already every bone in her body ached from the pounding they had been taking. Gray was right; the general was going to keep firing until he destroyed everything, including this planet.

Gray pulled her down on the floor. "Brace yourself, we're in for a rough ride."

Aki could see the massive alien creature spreading and expanding as Phantom after Phantom left it. It would soon cover them. She braced herself against a smooth panel, her feet against a second panel.

Gray was beside her, also braced, his strong hands holding her.

"Incoming," Dr. Sid's voice said. The sensors on the *Black Boa* gave them a few seconds warning, but nothing more. Dr. Sid had managed to get the ship out of the line of fire and on the ground near enough to the crater to help.

The world flashed white and the Quatro bounced hard. But Aki was so well braced this time she didn't end up with any more bruises.

Aki and Gray both stood quickly the moment the light passed, checking to make sure they were still in one piece. So far they were.

"Shield is holding," Gray said.

She could tell from the wonderful flowing gold around them.

"So any ideas?" she asked, turning to face the man she loved.

"Hang on and hope the general runs out of ammunition for that big cannon."

"And then what?"

He laughed. "If we're still alive at that point, we'll figure it out."

She looked out at the massive alien Gaia, now clearly bigger than just a few minutes before. If something didn't happen quickly, they were going to find themselves sitting inside that thing.

"Incoming!" Dr. Sid warned.

Gray and Aki dropped to the floor and got braced just in time to ride out still another shot from the cannon in the sky.

After the rocking had ended, Gray glanced at his watch. "The general has picked up the pace. Your speech helped a lot."

If they weren't in such trouble, she would have laughed.

He worked quickly to check the Quatro's systems. She sat there, not moving. She had expected she was going to die trying to get the eighth spirit, but now that spirit had been destroyed and taken back into the Gaia. And she was still going to die.

That just didn't feel right. Or fair.

She and Gray braced themselves as Dr. Sid warned them again.

This time the shaking was far, far worse, and the Quatro tipped and then rolled, end-over-end, more times than Aki wanted to think about.

When it finally came to rest, the Quatro was wedged between two steep rock faces, tipped slightly to the left. And much deeper into the cracks in the crater floor.

"You all right?" she asked Gray as they both looked around and did quick checks of the Quatro's systems.

"I've been better," he said, staring out at where they were.

Above them, the alien Gaia was a red, pulsating wall of energy. The last shot had opened massive cracks in the Earth, and the Quatro had fallen down into one of them, coming to rest twenty feet below the level of the alien Gaia.

"Man, we're in trouble now," Aki said, looking up at the red mass above them.

"More than you think," Gray said. "One more shot and I'm betting our shields will fail."

Aki had nothing to say about that.

The next moment Dr. Sid's voice filled the Quatro. "Incoming!"

chapter 25

General Hein watched the screen. He didn't much like what he was seeing. Not at all. The creature was now almost the size of the entire impact crater, and getting bigger with every shot from the Zeus cannon.

But maybe that meant it was getting weaker? That had to be what was going on. They were pounding it, smashing it, and when something got smashed, it spread out.

Major Sinn cleared his throat. "General, the system is overheating."

"I don't care," he said, staring at the monster below. "We're going to keep hitting it and hitting it, again and again, until it's dead."

"But, sir," the major protested, "we're not even sure if the cannon is having any effect on the creature."

Hein waved his arm at the screen. "And what do you call that? Can't you tell we're smashing it into a pulp?

This is our moment of victory. I order you to continue firing."

"Sir," the major said, "I'm sorry, but the automatic lock-out systems won't allow us to fire again. Not when it's this hot."

General Hein laughed. "I built this baby, I know what she can take. And I know when she can be fired."

He leaned forward and started keying in certain command codes on his board. Manual override codes.

"Stand ready," he said as he worked. "We're going back on the attack in just a few minutes."

The last shot from the Zeus cannon had knocked the Quatro even deeper into the fissure. And it had knocked out the Quatro's screens.

Gray pushed himself to his feet, then helped Aki to hers. She looked tired and beat up. A cut had opened on her arm and was bleeding pretty heavily.

"I'm all right," she said. "But I don't think we are." She pointed to the window.

Gray turned and stared. All he could see above them was the red and pink pulsation of the monster Phantom. And from the skin of that creature, other smaller Phantoms were starting to appear.

"We're sitting ducks in here," he said, shoving the hatch of the Quatro open and blocking it in that position. There was a rock ledge that the Quatro had landed on, and a small outcropping ten meters away that might give them shelter, if they could make it there in time.

Gray picked up two high-powered rifles and enough

charges to keep him firing for some time. Aki retrieved her communications equipment and attached it to her belt, then picked up a smaller rifle.

"Let's go," he said as he stepped out onto the rock ledge and helped her out.

Above them the pulsing, gigantic Phantom Gaia covered them like the roof of a stadium. Gray could have never imagined anything so large and yet living.

"This is not a good place to be," he said, staring at it as a small Phantom peeled off the side of the monster.

Aki pulled his sleeve gently and then pointed down into the massive crack in the Earth that plunged to one side of them. Gray could see a shimmering blue plasma. It was as if he were looking down into a deep, clear mountain lake.

"What is that?"

He looked at Aki. She was smiling, staring at it like she had just seen a newborn child.

"Wait," he said, looking back at the blue below them. "Don't tell me that's what I think it is."

"Yes," Aki said, her voice a whisper, as if she were in a very holy place. "That's Gaia."

Gray looked up at the red, alien Gaia over them, then down at the blue one below them. "This is *definitely* not a good place to be."

Suddenly Aki bent over, moaning as if in extreme pain.

"Hey, are you all right?"

He held her, keeping an eye out around them for moving Phantoms. General Hein hadn't fired again, which was both good news and bad. Without his cannon wiping out all the smaller Phantoms with every shot, the place was starting to get crowded again.

"I have to talk to Dr. Sid," Aki said, taking a deep breath and standing.

Gray took her communications link off her belt and handed it to her, then went back to guarding them.

"Dr. Sid," Aki said. "Do you read me?"

"Go ahead," he said. "I'm still here."

"You won't believe this," Aki said, "but right now we're standing on a ledge under the alien Gaia, looking down at the Earth's Gaia."

"What?"

Gray smiled. Dr. Sid was having as much trouble believing what they were seeing as they were. That was good to know.

"Gaia," Aki said. "It's right below us. I think that explains why the eighth spirit appeared here."

"Yes!" Gray heard the older scientist shout. "You're right! That's it! Hold on."

"Where does he expect we're going?" Gray asked.

Aki didn't even smile.

After a moment Dr. Sid's voice came back over the communications link. "I ran some calculations. From what I can tell, a single Phantom particle must have come into contact with a new spirit born from our own Gaia. If so, that would have given it the different energy signature that set it apart from the other Phantoms."

"Well," Gray said, watching as two Phantoms were born right overhead and moved off through the rock walls. "we're having a lot of births right now."

"You two could not have hoped for a better location to find a new, compatible spirit."

Gray again laughed. "He thinks this is great? He should be here."

"Whatever you do," Dr. Sid warned, "don't move. Stay right where you are while I see what I can track."

Gray watched a Phantom swooping in low from the right of the fissure. "Staying right where we are may not be as easy as it sounds."

Gray waited until he was sure the Phantom was going to move right through them, then he fired. The energy beam struck it and vaporized it.

"Don't shoot any of them!" Dr. Sid shouted over the comm link.

Aki shrugged, her face pale and sweat pouring off her forehead.

Dr. Sid kept up his lecture. "You could very well destroy our last hope."

"Then what do you suggest I do?" Gray asked, keeping an eye on three other Phantoms headed their way. "Ask them to play nice?"

"Combat strategy is your area of expertise, Captain, not mine. Just don't shoot any of them unless you absolutely have to."

Suddenly Aki turned, a sensor in her hand. She held it out, trying to scan around them. "Dr. Sid, I have a reading here in the fissure. Do you see it?"

"Yes," he said. "It's compatible. It must be very near you."

Aki moved back toward the hatch of the Quatro, following the reading on her sensor.

Gray kept a sharp eye on the half dozen Phantoms

headed their way. "Well, Doc," he shouted, hoping Dr. Sid would hear him over Aki's com link. "Which one is it?"

Aki shook her head, seeming to be almost in a trance.

Gray watched as the Phantoms moved closer. He didn't have much time if he was going to stop them all.

"It's getting crowded down here."

Neither Aki or Dr. Sid answered him.

He glanced around. Aki had slumped in the hatchway of the Quatro.

She looked dead.

"Aki!" he shouted, the panic raising in his stomach.

She didn't move.

"Aki!

No response.

She couldn't be dead. Maybe she had just passed out again, as she had done in the wasteland.

He turned back to face the oncoming Phantoms.

He had no choice any more. It was either them or him, and with Aki laying there like that, maybe already dead, he just didn't have much choice.

Using his shots carefully, he picked off the closest Phantoms one by one.

It didn't seem to do any good. They just kept coming.

chapter 26

The dream was back.

The same alien sun and large moon hung in the sky. Aki looked around at the destroyed alien landscape. It was at a point in the dream where the two armies were already fighting, but before the wall of fire came and took everything.

But this dream was different.

Very different.

The live armies were gone. Only the empty, gray landscape remained.

Why had the dream changed? What did it mean?

Suddenly the alien particles she had carried for a long time burst out of her chest and swirled in the air in front of her.

Then, as if directed, they burrowed into the dead ground and disappeared.

Aki could not believe what she was seeing.

Green grass and flowers started to grow around her feet, spreading outward over the hills. Everywhere she looked, life was coming back.

Then she awoke.

Gray was standing just a few feet away from her, firing his rifle as fast as he could, keeping the Phantoms at bay. For the moment he seemed to be winning.

She opened her shirt and looked at the holographic image of the alien particles trapped in her chest. The membrane was still there, but the alien particles had vanished. In their place was a complete spirit wave.

"I have it!" she shouted. And she knew exactly what had happened.

"Aki?" Gray said, turning toward her. "Are you all right?"

He turned back and fired at another nearby Phantom.

"Gray, can you come in here closer?" she asked. "I need you." Then she called for Dr. Sid. She was going to need his help as well.

Gray backed toward her, never taking his eye off the closest Phantom.

"Dr. Sid, are you there? The wave pattern is complete. It happened in the dream. It was the dream."

"That is wonderful," he said, his voice clear.

Aki rigged up a wire from her chest plate to the Quatro com system, downloading the information she had to Dr. Sid. "Data coming in. The spirit found me, Doctor."

Gray killed two more Phantoms before Dr. Sid's voice came back strong. "Oh, my word," he said, clearly looking at the data she had sent him from her chest plate. "I see it now. How logical."

Gray fired again, vaporizing another Phantom, then turned. "Well, I don't understand. What is going on?"

Aki turned and started to work on the equipment just inside the Quatro door. "Give me an ovo-pack," she said. "I need to power up the shield."

"But we'll be defenseless," Gray said, looking at the last ovo-pack in his rifle. Aki could tell it was the last one. His other rifle lay discarded on the ground a few feet away.

"Just do it," she said.

Gray pulled the ovo-pack out of his rifle and handed it to her.

"Get in," she said, moving as fast as she could to get the shield up and running.

Gray climbed in and sat, alternately watching her and the Phantoms that were coming closer and closer. "I hope you know what you are doing."

"I do," she said, slapping the shield back to on position, hoping it would kick on quickly. "We have to project the completed wave from me out into the alien Gaia."

"What?" Gray asked.

"Dr. Sid's theory was right," she said.

"Thank you," Dr. Sid said over the com line.

"I'm cured. I have the eighth spirit."

"Are you sure?" Gray asked as she got the last wire in place and hit the control for the shield to turn it on.

"I'm sure," she said.

"But how could you know that?"

"A dream told me."

He turned and looked at her, still clearly puzzled as she worked as fast as she could.

Around them the shield kicked on just as a Phantom slammed into the side of the Quatro. Sparks flew, but the golden, shimmering shield held.

"That was what I call close," he said. "I thought you were dead."

"I might have been," she said, pulling him toward her and reaching up to pull his head down for a kiss. "But does this feel dead?"

He couldn't answer her, but she was pretty sure of his response.

After a moment she pulled away. "Now we have work to do."

It took them ten more minutes, with some help from Dr. Sid, before they got the energy wave just the way they needed it, taken from her and put out through the Quatro's shield to the alien Gaia.

"Ready?" she asked.

"I've been ready for years," Gray said, checking over the control board in front of him.

Aki hit the switch and watched as, outside the Quatro, the new wave slowly started to purify the Phantom Gaia, turning it from an angry red to a wonderful, peaceful blue.

The same blue Aki was sure it had started out as, before all the fighting, before the destruction, before the long eons trapped in space.

Before the alien Gaia had become so angry.

Now it would only be a matter of time, and the alien Gaia would be at rest.

A moment later Aki realized they didn't have the time.

"Incoming!"

Dr. Sid's warning filled the small Quatro.

"Oh, no," she said.

Gray yanked her to the floor, covering her and protecting her with his body as around them the world shook.

And then came apart.

General Hein sat in his command chair, watching the Zeus cannon fire on the alien creature in the crater. It had taken him longer than he had wanted to override the safety controls to get this shot. But now he wasn't going to let up until the creature was gone from the face of the planet.

"Warning! System overload!"

"Would someone shut off that computer?" Hein shouted, not taking his attention from the screen and his target.

"Can't, sir," the major said.

"Warning! System overload."

"We need to stop firing, sir!" Major Sinn yelled over the computer voice.

"No!" Hein said. He studied his board. He had complete control of the firing and he was going to keep at it.

"Warning! System overload!"

"It must be done!" Hein shouted, keeping the beam firing into the creature. He wasn't going to let up until it was gone, no matter what damage it caused to this weapon. The damage could be fixed after the alien Phantoms were gone.

"Warning! Warning! Warning!"

"Contain that, Major," Hein said, "whatever the problem is."

The Major said nothing.

One soldier from the back of the room shouted, "Major, we have ovo-packs staring to react."

"General, we must shut down!"

"Warning! Warning! Warning! All personnel to emergency evacuation posts."

Suddenly the weapon shut down.

General Hein stared at the screen. The alien was still there.

He stabbed at the controls on the panel in front of him, trying to get the cannon to fire again.

"Warning! All personnel report to evacuation posts at once."

General Hein turned to stare at Major Sinn. "What is that blasted computer talking about?"

Sinn just pointed out the side port at the ovo-pack containment area of the station. As Hein watched, the entire section of the station exploded.

The station rocked and then went dark. Hein barely kept himself in his command chair.

A moment later the emergency power came back up, followed by the screens and control boards. Maybe not all was lost.

Major Sinn righted himself and looked at the general. "You've killed us all, you know?"

"How do you mean that, Major?"

The station again shook.

This time the explosion was closer and harder.

Major Sinn did not answer.

Another explosion shut the lights off for good and rocked the command area like a hard earthquake.

This time Hein didn't manage to stay in his chair.

He flew across the room in the zero g, smashing into a control panel.

A moment later, the last explosion ripped the entire station apart.

General Hein didn't even know what hit him.

Below the station, the angry red colors of the alien Gaia pulsed and surged and expanded out of the crater.

chapter 27

Aki came to lying faceup on the rock surface, one arm dangling over the fissure that lead down to the Earth's Gaia. Her head hurt and her back hurt, and she was bleeding from both elbows and a dozen other cuts and scrapes.

But she was still alive.

She pushed herself to her feet and looked up. The alien Gaia was red and angry-looking over her. The wave they had started had been stopped by the firing of the cannon. At least for the moment, the smaller Phantoms were not around. But she had no doubt they would be soon.

Aki turned to see if she could see Gray and the Quatro. Then she understood how she had gotten outside of it. The machine had been smashed and crumpled.

Panic washed through her. He couldn't be in there. No one could survive in that kind of twisted metal.

"Gray!" She started to run toward the wreck when she saw him leaning against a rock ten meters away. Quickly she scrambled to him.

The closer she got, the more she could tell he was hurt badly. Blood was dripping out of the corner of his mouth, and his eyes were rolled up into his head. His breathing was shallow and raspy. He clearly had internal injuries.

"Gray!" she shouted as she knelt beside him. "Don't leave me, Gray!"

His head rolled forward and he opened his eyes slowly. A weak smile followed when he saw her. "I told Dr. Sid this was a one-way trip. Looks like I was right."

Aki held him against her, trying to keep him conscious. She couldn't let him go. He couldn't die.

She searched around her for any sign of the communications link she had been carrying. It was nowhere to be found. And even if she could find it, Dr. Sid couldn't get the ship down there through that Gaia.

"Well," he said, his head rolling a little. "This feels like a fine time to leave. I love you, you know."

"I know," she said, holding him even tighter. "But you can't leave. Hang on, please. I need you!"

"Aki," he said, closing his eyes. "Don't."

"No, listen to me," she said, not letting him talk. "I've still got the alien wave inside of me. I need your help getting it into the alien Gaia."

His eyes opened again, and he looked at her, blinking in a effort to clear away the fog.

"That's right," she said. "I still have it. All I need to do is reach up and touch the alien. The wave inside me will transfer."

Aki looked at him. His eyes were there, his mind for the moment was there. She could see that. But the pain was clearly bad for him. She had to get him help. "Hold on, Gray. Help will come for you as soon as I'm done."

"No!" he said, his voice firm. "I'm not going to make it, Aki."

"You're going to make it." She couldn't let him talk like that. He had to stay positive.

"We both know that isn't true," he said. He looked past her at the angry alien above them. Then he moved, trying to get into a position where he could get up.

"But I have an idea on how we can solve this and you can get out of here. Help me stand."

"I don't think—"

"Help me." The command in his voice was back, and strong. "We need to make it to the edge."

She looked over her shoulder at what he had seen, then started to understand what he was trying to do. "Gray, please."

"Listen to me," he said, leaning against her as his legs gained strength under him. "You saved my life once. Now I want you to save yourself. And this world."

Gray held her around the shoulders, his weight against her. Then he turned her and together they moved to the edge of the massive crack in the ground. Below them the wonderful blue of the Earth's Gaia was welcoming. Above was the angry, swirling red of the alien, expanding out and coming closer and closer every moment.

He pointed down to a ledge a few feet below where they were. "Jump down there and hold onto me."

"Gray, no!" she said. She couldn't handle the thought of being without him.

"Let me do this, Aki," he said. "You have to trust me."

He looked into her eyes, and she saw complete love. She did trust him. She just couldn't lose him.

"Don't leave me, Gray."

He laughed, then coughed up more blood before going on. "You've been trying to tell me from the first day we met that death isn't the end. Don't back out on me now."

She looked at him as he smiled.

"Now that I finally believe."

He motioned that she should jump down onto the shelter of the lower rock ledge.

She did as she was told, landing on the ledge hard. Then she reached back up and touched his leg, holding onto him. She knew what he was doing was right, yet she didn't want it to happen. There had to be another way.

One of the tentacles of the alien Gaia was swinging back and forth over his head.

He looked down at her as the angry red of the alien swept toward him.

"I love you," he said.

The next moment the alien Gaia's tentacle smashed into him.

And then through him.

His blue energy merged with the energy inside of her, pulling the wave out of her and up and into the alien Gaia.

For an instant, they were one.

Joined forever.

Then he was gone, his body slumped to the rock surface, dead.

"Gray!" she shouted, her scream echoing through the fissure.

It was sudden and clear, what was happening.

Gray had used his body to transfer the completed wave inside of her to the alien Gaia.

Now the light particles of the completed spirit wave swirled the alien Gaia into a wonderful whirlwind of blue color.

The color twisted upward, converting more and more of the angry Gaia as it went.

Higher and higher into the sky the beautiful blue energy flew.

Aki could feel it radiating from the Gaia. Love, understanding, peace.

The red of the anger was being transformed.

Aki watched as the Gaia slowly became a vertical river of blue and greens and silvers, all swirling upward toward the heavens.

The alien Gaia was leaving.

It had finally attained the peace it had never had on its homeworld. It was now going home again.

Aki watched until there wasn't a particle of blue or green or silver left to be seen in the sky. Then she climbed up onto the ledge above and stood at the edge of the fissure, next to Gray's body.

Below her the blue of the Earth's Gaia was slowly settling back into the ground. She knew Gray was there now. He had died to save the planet.

She would make sure he was never forgotten.

It took her a while to slowly climb up the side of the crater toward where Dr. Sid and the *Black Boa* were. Her shoulder ached, and she was bleeding from a dozen small cuts. But somehow she had to get out of there.

She looked back down the side of the crater. They were going to have to go back and get Gray's body and give it a hero's burial. But there would be time for that later.

Finally she reached the top edge and sat down to rest on the hard rock outcropping that looked out over the impact crater. The sun was slowly coming out from behind some clouds. The Zeus cannon had made the crater deeper, and destroyed the asteroid the alien had arrived on. Yet now the crater didn't look as dead, as ruined as it had when she and Gray went down into it.

Over her head a hawk circled. Its cry made her look up at the wonderful blue sky. The clouds were gone and the warm sun was shining. Not the heat of the alien sun, or the desert sun, but the comfort of a life-giving warmth. It felt good on her shoulders.

Below her feet a weed was growing out of a rock, sprouting so fast she could see it grow.

She looked around. Life of all kinds was taking hold again, sprouting as if pouring from the ground. Even in the impact crater she could see the green of weeds exploding in life from the barren earth that just a few hours before had held the anger of an entire alien planet's Gaia.

The hawk cried again over her head, reminding her she had to move, to get things done that needed to be done.

"All right," she said, pushing herself to her feet. A few hundred meters away, Dr. Sid was coming out of the hatch of the *Black Boa*. He knelt at once and studied the ground. Even from this distance, she could see the carpet of green springing up around the ship. She had to admit that, after all the years of always worrying about being killed by a Phantom, it felt strange to walk outside like this.

And even stranger to see green grass and plants growing wild.

She had no doubt it would take everyone time to learn again how to go into the fields and the mountains without fear. But the human race would eventually come out of its shell and live the life the planet was offering.

Gray had given the human race a great gift. He had given everyone back *life*.

Clearly, death was not the end. In Gray's case it was the beginning.

About the Author

Dean Wesley Smith has written over sixty novels, among them the blockbuster novelization of the *X-Men* movie and a brand-new *Spider-Man* novel. Dean has been nominated for every major award in science fiction and fantasy, and has won the World Fantasy Award. In *Star Trek*, besides collaborating with Kristine Kathryn Rusch on the *Star Trek: Voyager* novels *Shadow* and *Echoes*, Dean has also written the *Captain Proton* novel, the original script for *Star Trek: Klingon*, and the very first *Star Trek: SCE* e-book, as well as books with two other authors. He also currently edits the ongoing *Star Trek: Strange New Worlds* new-writer anthologies.